✳ MISTER FRED ✳

Mister Fred

JILL PINKWATER

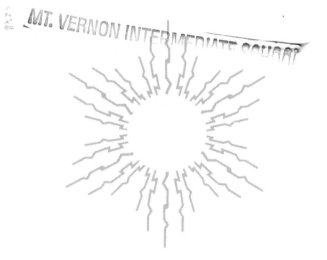

Dutton Children's Books

* NEW YORK *

Library of Congress Cataloging-in-Publication Data

Pinkwater, Jill. Mister Fred / by Jill Pinkwater—1st ed. p. cm.

SUMMARY: The children of class 6-A suspect their new teacher of
being a telepathic space alien. ISBN 0-525-44778-4 [1. Schools—Fiction.
2. Teachers—Fiction. 3. Extraterrestrial beings—Fiction. 4. Extrasensory
perception—Fiction.] I. Title. II. Title: Mr. Fred. PZ7.P6336Mi
1994 [Fic]—dc20 93-42938 CIP AC

Published in the United States by
Dutton Children's Books, a division of Penguin Books USA Inc.
375 Hudson Street, New York, New York 10014
Designed by Adrian Leichter
Printed in U.S.A.
FIRST EDITION
1 3 5 7 9 10 8 6 4 2

FOR DANIEL

AND ALL THOSE OTHER GOOD

TEACHERS WHO ARE PRETENDING

TO BE EARTHLINGS

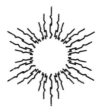

✳ CONTENTS ✳

✳ MISTER FRED ✳

It Was the Best of Times—Almost

1

It had been the best day of my life, a perfect Friday—the first week of school. The sun was shining. The air was crisp. A few leaves on the biggest trees had begun to change color. Miss Cintron, champion sixth-grade teacher of My Dear Watson Elementary School was *my* teacher. A couple of good friends were in my class, *and* that morning I, Anya Murray, formerly a nobody, had been elected class president of 6-A. I couldn't see how life could get much better.

The lunch bell rang. "Grab your outer garments and follow me!" Miss Cintron wrapped her sweater around her shoulders and marched toward the door.

"Where do you think we're going Anya?" asked Arthur, my friend, next-door neighbor, and class sergeant-at-arms.

"How should I know?"

"You're class president."

"For almost a *whole* half hour. I know nothing." I grabbed my windbreaker off my hook just in time to see Miss Cintron leave the room.

"We're going to lose her!" someone warned. The class surged forward and got tangled together in a clump of desks, chairs, and outer garments.

"Class!" Miss Cintron stuck her head into the room. "Stop playing around. Anya, why don't you get them moving?"

"Me?"

"You're their new leader."

"I am?" I said, stumbling over the leg of an overturned chair.

"Presidents are supposed to lead. Get used to it. Now let's get going before everything burns." Miss Cintron left for the second time.

"Burns?"

"How come she came back for us?"

"It's too warm for sweaters."

"So leave yours where it is."

"I didn't bring one today."

"Why are you discussing this? Keep moving," I directed, pushing my way to the front of the room. Everyone was talking, and only a couple of kids had gotten free of the mob.

"But she *never* comes back for us. It's part of the rules. Let go of my sweater!"

"So what? They're her rules. She can change them. Get off the floor!"

"Get off my foot."

"I'm out of here!" I called over my shoulder as I freed myself from the crush and headed for the hall. I was almost run over by a couple of my faster classmates.

There was the usual bumping and noise as we rushed down the stairway after Miss Cintron. Miss Cintron was the only teacher at My Dear Watson who didn't believe in keeping students in straight lines—except during fire drills, of course. The first thing she ever explained to us had to do with our getting from one place to another.

"Sixth graders are on the cusp of adolescence—almost young adults. Herding you around like trained horses will not teach you independence or help you mature. When I move out of this room, it will be your responsibility to follow me. Do not knock each other down. Do not raise your voices. Do not terrorize the smaller children in the school. Do not vandalize property. Never run in the hallways. Arrive at our destination no more than twenty seconds after me, and we will get along splendidly. Oh yes, one last thing: If you get separated from the group, do not expect me to take valuable time to search for you."

We liked being treated as almost young adults but found there were two problems we had to face every time we left the room. The first was that Miss Cintron *never* told us where we were headed. The second was that Miss Cintron was the fastest walker any of us had ever seen —plus she was able to go up or down any staircase two steps at a time.

In order to keep her in sight without breaking into a dead run, we had to be constantly alert. If you turned your head to talk to someone or stopped to tie a shoe or get a drink of water, you would miss her ducking around a corner or going through an unexpected doorway. Our school is not that big, but during the first two days of the term, there were quite a few kids who missed some important activities because they couldn't find where the class had gone.

I, myself, never got to the science lesson on fungi— which took place at Miss Cintron's secret mushroom garden in a basement storage room. But by day four, when Miss Cintron taught the first lesson of her special yearlong course called "Survival 101: Taking Care of Yourself," we had all become experts at keeping right on her heels. Not a single kid missed "F•U•N•E•X? (that's EF-YOO-EN-EE-X, get it?) Break 'em, boil 'em, fry 'em, eat 'em!" which took place in the school kitchen. We each got a Chef d'Oeuf certificate (that's "egg cook" in French)—with our specialties noted in purple ink. Mine read: "Oeufs Brouillés Extraordinaires"—extraordinary scrambled eggs.

Keeping Miss Cintron in sight meant adventure and fun.

So there we were, on that perfect Friday, trying our hardest to keep up with her. We arrived on the ground floor seconds behind Miss Cintron—but the goofing around upstairs had thrown off our timing. Miss Cintron had disappeared. Everyone was out of breath—which didn't stop them from chattering like crows.

"I don't see her."

"She lost an entire class."

"An entire class lost her."

"We messed up."

"Anya, *you* lost her."

"I did not."

"You *did*!"

"Right, it's Anya's fault."

"Why is it *my* fault?"

"You're president."

"She went left."

"No, right."

"Do you think she'll start with the whole class missing?"

"Start what?"

"The out-of-classroom activity."

"But it's lunchtime."

"What does that mean?"

"Are you stupid?"

"SHUT UP!" I shouted.

"YOU SHUT UP!" a couple of my classmates shouted back at me.

"SHE'S OUTSIDE. FOLLOW ME!" I shouted again and headed for the door to the playground.

"You're making that up!"

"I'm your leader. Trust me."

"Why?"

"Because I smell meat cooking," I explained.

"So what. It's lunchtime."

"I said that already."

"School lunch is pizza today," I explained further.

"So what. Where's Miss Cintron?"

I put my hands over my ears and wondered if being a leader was always so annoying. I couldn't make a move without everyone asking me a million questions. I hoped I was right and that Miss Cintron was waiting for us on the other side of the door. If I was wrong, I'd probably be impeached on the spot. I pushed open the door. The class rushed forward, practically lifting me off my feet as we landed outside.

"Surprise!" Miss Cintron and a couple of people I

didn't recognize were standing behind a table loaded with food. The wind blew the smells from a smoking barbecue into our faces. Everyone started talking again.

"This is great!"

"What a teacher."

"I can't wait for next week."

"Why don't you finish enjoying this week?"

We stuffed ourselves until we couldn't move. I was chewing my last bite of hot dog and thinking how great everything had worked out. At My Dear Watson, every kid learned about Miss Cintron the first week of kindergarten and spent the next six years hoping to get her as a teacher. On the last day of fifth grade, when everyone got a little yellow note assigning classrooms and teachers for the following year and yours said you would be spending sixth grade in the double room on the top floor of the school with Miss Cintron, it was like winning the lottery.

"I have some good news I'd like to share with you." Miss Cintron smiled at us. We smiled back at her.

"I have been chosen to participate in the Argentinian teacher-exchange program—a great honor for me."

"Hey!"

"Wow!"

"So we're celebrating."

"Do you get to be on television?"

"Do you get prize money?"

My classmates and I were applauding our honored teacher.

"No, no, please class. I don't think you understand." Miss Cintron was blushing. "This isn't a celebration party. It's a good-bye party. I'm flying to Buenos Aires on Sunday."

"Doesn't that mean you'll miss school Monday?" I asked, already planning to have a headache, which would keep me home until Miss Cintron returned.

"I don't think I'm making myself clear. I'm going to teach in Argentina—in a little village—for at least a year. It's something I've wanted to do for a very long time, and my chance has finally come."

There was sudden, absolute silence on the playground. Kids stopped chewing. They stopped moving. I think some stopped breathing for a few seconds. I felt as if someone had hit me in the stomach.

"So, what you're saying is that you're leaving us—for good," I said.

"Shut up, Anya," someone sobbed.

The rest of the day was awful. Kids sulked and cried and got angry but, in the end, made a huge hug circle around Miss Cintron and almost smothered her with love.

"We'll get her to come back," I vowed to Arthur as we walked home.

"How?"

"I don't know, but we will."

10

✳

"One day as president and you're turning into a real politician," Arthur grumbled.

"What do you mean by that?"

"Making promises you can't keep."

"We *will* get her to come back."

"And eggs grow on trees."

Nobody Likes a Sixth Grader

2

Class 6-A became a legend at My Dear Watson Elementary School. We were clever. We were sneaky. We were bad. We were *very bad*. We were a team. We had a plan. It was working.

Five weeks passed. Seven substitute teachers had come, seen, and given up. Once again it was a Friday. We had made it through another week without Miss Cintron. The word was out. No sane teacher would accept permanent assignment to our class.

"Two twenty-seven, exactly." Mike Carson, our official timekeeper, shouted to be heard above the ear-clogging noise in the room.

Alice Greenbaum, our class secretary and queen of the spitballs, noted it in the class log.

"Did you record his name?" yelled Kathy Pepper, the class nitpicker. Alice raised her blowgun straw to her mouth and a spitball flew right to the tip of Kathy's nose.

"Arrgh, that's disgusting," Kathy shrieked.

Susan Ames had been working on an enormous wad of bubble gum. When Kathy yelled, a huge bubble broke, leaving pink gum all over Susan's face and bangs.

"I'm going to get you, Kathy," she threatened.

"I didn't do anything; it was Alice," Kathy defended herself as Susan got out of her seat.

A couple of the boys began a race around the edge of the room. Two kids were drawing suspicious pictures on the chalkboard.

"Are you sure that teacher is really gone?" asked Louise Sinbad.

"Do you see him here?" I asked.

"He could come back, you know. He could bring Pomeroy."

"Old Bad Breath might show up, but he won't have that man with him. You heard what he said just before he slammed the door." I smiled at the memory.

"Yeah—a person had to be out of his head to even think about teaching sixth graders. Do you think he thinks we're regular sixth graders? What if nobody outside this room realizes what's going on?" Bettina Gomez sounded worried.

"How could they not realize?" Kathy asked. "My sister says that when we get going, they can hear us at the junior high."

"I mean realize what we want—what will make us act normal again," Bettina explained.

"They know what we want. Stop worrying," I said.

"What are you talking about? I can't hear you. How can I take notes if I don't know what's going on?" Alice shouted. She slapped the class log down on her desk for emphasis.

I couldn't answer Alice because the noise level had reached the critical point. The window panes were shaking. One more high-pitched scream and they would shatter into a million pieces. There were now four kids racing around the room. Alice, Susan, Kathy, and Bettina were yelling at each other, a couple of kids had overturned desks and were choosing sides for some kind of battle, and the rest looked like they were about to really lose it in a big way.

"A state of chaos!" Ellenbeth Maggin shouted in my ear.

"What's chaos?" I asked.

"This," she said, waving her arm at the room.

"I've got to stop them," I said.

"Chaos can't be stopped," Ellenbeth giggled as she joined a group of noisy friends.

"You wanna bet? ARTHUR!" I grabbed hold of his arm as he raced past me.

"What do you want, Anya? I'm busy." Arthur struggled to free himself.

"We have to stop them."

"Why? This is fun."

"We're not supposed to be having fun; we're supposed to be executing our plan, Arthur."

"What plan?" Arthur looked confused for a minute. "Oh, right, *that* plan. *Your* plan you mean. Have you noticed it isn't working?" He shook my hand loose from his arm.

"It *is* working. We've chased away seven substitute teachers. One lasted less than a day. Soon they'll have to make Miss Cintron come home to teach us. They'll have no choice. *She'll* have no choice."

"WOULD YOU LIKE TO BET ON THAT, MISS MURRAY?" Mr. Pomeroy's booming voice seemed to hit my head like a blow. He had snuck into the room and was standing right behind us. Arthur and I began moving away, but the evil principal grabbed our shirt collars. No one else noticed he was there.

"STOP! Now!" Pomeroy ordered. The class froze in place.

"Aha! Chaos can be stopped after all—by the Pomeroy Method of brute force." In the suddenly silent room, Ellenbeth's voice rang out like a bell.

"WHO SAID THAT?" Pomeroy demanded. "Never mind. I've had it with you—all of you. You are the mangiest bunch of incorrigible delinquents I have ever had the misfortune to know."

"Is that good or bad?" asked Helene Holman, my best friend.

Pomeroy glared at her. Then he looked at our innocent, attentive faces. "Today was the end of it. You drove away yet another substitute—a fine man—a good teacher—a brave man willing to walk into this pit of hell."

There were gasps and oh's and sucked-in breaths all over the room. My classmates were having a whole lot more fun than they were supposed to be having. I was afraid that Arthur wasn't the only one who had forgotten why we had become the Class from Hell.

"Do you know how many substitute teachers you've destroyed this semester?" Everyone nodded, but Pomeroy went on anyway. "Six. No, counting today, seven. *Seven* teachers in five weeks. Seven good people refusing to return to our school unless we guarantee that they never have to face a sixth-grade class again. How do you expect me to find a permanent replacement for Miss Cintron if you behave like beasts?"

"You can't replace Miss Cintron," someone said from behind a hand.

"Make her come back!" An angry voice demanded.

"We want Miss Cintron. WE WANT MISS CINTRON! WE WANT MISS CINTRON! NO JUSTICE, NO PEACE! NO JUSTICE, NO PEACE!" My classmates were stamping their feet and clapping their hands. They were back on track. They hadn't completely forgotten our mission.

Pomeroy looked disgusted. He had seen and heard us demonstrate many times before. "MISS CINTRON IS NOT COMING BACK—NO MATTER WHAT YOU DO! YOU CAN STAND ON YOUR HEADS. YOU CAN TURN YOURSELVES INSIDE OUT. NOTHING WILL WORK!"

The class became quiet. Pomeroy had said the same things before, but each time we heard them, we got depressed.

"And furthermore, I am your principal. You will begin to show more respect for me and my office. You will stop referring to me as Pomeroy or Old Bad Breath. I am *Mister* Pomeroy, and I most certainly do *not* have bad breath.

"If I had my way, there would be a separate sixth-grade school—other districts have them. Isolate the pre-adolescents—let them find their way to their teens without bothering anyone else." Pomeroy had a peaceful look on his face.

Then a spitball whizzed past his head. "That's it. I'm going to my office to have yet another note to your parents copied. I will be gone exactly five minutes. Straighten the desks and chairs in this room. If you are not all sitting, hands folded, in your proper places when I return, the entire class will get detention until Christmas." Pomeroy left the room.

"Did you have to do that, Alice?" Mike complained as he righted his desk.

"Do what?" asked Alice, innocently, as she packed her blowgun straw in her bookbag.

"It was funny," said Helene, moving a chair into place.

Alice put the class log on her desk and opened it. "Now, how long was this last one with us?"

We had agreed never to speak the names of the temporary teachers sent to replace Miss Cintron.

"Twenty-nine hours and twenty-seven minutes," I said. Math is my best subject.

Alice wrote in the log and flipped a few pages. "We're slowing down," she said.

"Maybe they're getting tougher substitutes."

"Maybe they're warning each other. This one checked his chair before sitting down on Monday."

"Maybe. We have to come up with some new tactics."

"You think they're going to give us another one?"

"They have to. It's the law. We get substitutes until they find us a permanent teacher."

"What permanent teacher would teach us?"

"Miss Cintron."

"She's different. She actually likes us."

"We never tried to destroy her."

"She'd like us anyway."

"You're nuts."

I interrupted the conversation. "Look, we stick to our plan. When we write telling her nobody will teach us, she'll come home."

"They won't give us her address."

"She's been sending us postcards. Sooner or later she'll send a letter with a return address on it. When we get it, we'll send her a telegram. We have to hold out until then."

Pomeroy walked into the room. "It's a good thing you're in your seats. The notes to your parents, guardians, or keepers will be arriving in a few minutes. In the meantime, take out your books."

"Which books?" I asked.

"Don't smart mouth me, Miss Anya Murray."

"I wasn't . . . ," I began, grabbing my bookbag strap.

We were practiced clock-watchers—especially on Fridays. The instant the minute hand clicked onto the twelve, we were out of our seats and moving. The school bell covered up the sound of the classroom door slamming open against the wall.

"DON'T THINK YOU'RE GETTING AWAY WITH ANYTHING! I'M MAILING THOSE NOTES TO YOUR HOMES!"

"You know what the problem is . . . ," I said to Arthur on the way home.

"What problem?"

"Sixth grade is supposed to be the greatest year of elementary school. You're on top. You're the seniors. You're almost teenagers. You're taller than the other kids—also stronger. Your mind is better than it's ever been because you know more—you can think better. And all the other kids in school wish they were sixth graders."

"Like I said, what problem?" Arthur asked.

"The problem is that nobody actually likes a sixth grader except other sixth graders."

"And parents," said Arthur.

"I wouldn't bet on that," I said, thinking of Pomeroy stuffing twenty-five nasty notes into a mailbox.

"Miss Cintron likes sixth graders," said Arthur.

"I wonder if she's the only one."

"Only one what?"

"The only person in the world who is not a sixth grader—and actually likes them."

Mr. Fred, a Piece of Cake

3

I beat my mother to the mail on Saturday morning. In with the bills and junk flyers was Pomeroy's letter. I knew it would be. Nothing takes more than a day to get delivered in Washingtonville. We have one post office. Mail arrives, mail is delivered. Hardly anything ever gets lost. Usually that's something to be happy about.

The envelope containing my doom wasn't quite sealed. I thought about taking it into the garage, prying up the flap, and reading the note—just to see how much trouble I was in so I could prepare myself. Maybe I could even hide it for the weekend. I was about to shove the letter under my shirt when my mother rushed out of the house.

She kissed me on the top of my head, grabbed the mail from my hand, and headed for the car.

"See you in about an hour, Anya—unless you want to come food shopping with me."

"No thanks, Mom. I think I'll do some laundry."

"You'll what?" My mother looked at me suspiciously. Then she flipped through the mail. My mother is a sharp lady.

I walked casually toward the house. "Stop. Stand still. Do not move a muscle." My mother ripped open the envelope. She read the note, shoved it into her purse, and sighed loudly. "Explain!" she said.

"How can I explain if I don't know what Old Bad Breath said about me?"

"Don't call your principal 'Old Bad Breath,' and how did you know this was from him?"

"I saw the return address?"

"The return address was just that—the address of your school. Mr. Pomeroy's name was *not* on the envelope. Get in the car. You're coming with me. We'll talk while I shop."

I groaned but did as I was told. My mother hates wasting time. We usually wind up doing two or even three things at once—like cleaning the house while practicing for a spelling test—or doing laundry while cooking dinner *and* going over my math homework. My mother says single parents should have eight arms like an octopus and a machine to slow down time to make their lives easier.

It was not our jolliest shopping trip. The letter from Old Bad Breath didn't mention me personally, so at first I thought I had a chance. Between the vegetables and the deli counter, I tried to convince my mother that I was just an innocent bystander—a victim of my classmates' enthusiasm. By the time we reached the frozen foods, my mother had gotten me to admit that maybe I had joined my classmates in making a tiny little bit of trouble. We were whizzing through the dairy section when my own dear mother called me a known instigator, a classroom terrorist, and a menace to hardworking substitutes. My mother *always* takes the side of working people. In the checkout line, my mother complained about having to take time to go to another meeting between Pomeroy and the parents of 6-A. "This is the sixth note I've gotten this term. It will be the fourth meeting in five weeks."

"So don't go. Tell him you're busy—which you are," I suggested helpfully as I piled cans of cat food in a bag.

"Hah!" said my mother and glared at me.

"What does that mean?" I asked. My mother turned her back to me and rushed to the car.

On the way home, my mother reminded me that, as class president, it was my job to set a good example for my fellow sixth graders. It was time for me to stop being a ringleader and start being a mensch. I promised I would try. As we drove into our driveway, my mother forgave me. The rest of the weekend was uneventful.

On Monday morning, I met Arthur for our usual walk to school.

"Did you get in trouble?" I asked. Arthur stared at me blankly. "About the note from Old Bad Breath," I explained.

"No," said Arthur, smiling. "I told my parents it was mostly your fault. They believed me."

"That's rotten," I said.

"You're class president. Besides, you've been getting me into trouble since we were four years old. They said you're a menace."

"My mother kind of said the same thing. She wants me to be a mensch."

"What's a mensch?"

"Someone who is nice and good and helpful and kind—an upright citizen."

"Not possible," said Arthur.

"I know." The light turned green, and we were off to begin another exciting week at My Dear Watson Elementary School, probably the only school in the United States named after a deceased pencil manufacturer. Mrs. Watson, president of the school board, donated the money to add a gym and cafeteria onto the old Arrandale School. Her only condition was that the school be renamed My

Dear Watson after her husband who, in life, she usually called, 'Watson, you idiot!' No amount of arguing or persuasion would get her to name the school Watson Elementary or even Joseph Watson Elementary. It was a take-it-or-leave-it deal. The town took it.

Arthur and I arrived at the school playground to find most of the classes had already entered the building. We ran upstairs.

"There's nobody here," announced Alice, noting the date and time in the class log.

"*We're* all here," said Mike.

"I meant adults. There are no adults here."

"We know what you meant. I think they've run out of substitute teachers. Our plan worked. We've won." As president, I had led my classmates to a great victory— despite the opinion of my mother.

The good feelings lasted about a minute. Then our whole world changed—forever. The door opened and a man wandered into the room. He moved slowly, in little circles, as he looked at the ceiling, the floor, the windows, the chalkboard, the maps on the wall, the clock. As he corkscrewed around the room, his head bobbed up and down and from side to side like some kind of mechanical toy. Finally he reached the teacher's desk. He put down the stack of books and papers he was carrying and turned his attention to us.

He stood in front of the desk in his green-and-red-plaid

sports jacket, pink bow tie, black-and-white checked pants which were a little too short, red socks, and blue suede shoes. His greasy hair was plastered to his head. He wore bottle-thick, black-rimmed, perfectly round eyeglasses. He looked at each one of us in turn—straight in the eyes. As his eyes grabbed ours, his head bobbed and his ears wiggled. Naturally we began to giggle. So did he. The giggles were becoming belly laughs when Pomeroy marched into the room.

"What is going on here?" he demanded.

"We are getting acquainted, dear sir," said the man.

"The little monsters aren't giving you any trouble are they?" Pomeroy growled.

"The little monsters are trouble-free at the moment." The man's hands gestured toward us. His long fingers seemed to have a life of their own.

"Then I'll leave you to it. Remember what I told you about them. Good luck." Pomeroy began to walk out of the room. Then, stopping himself midstep, he stared into the hall and spoke, "This is your new teacher—new *permanent* teacher. No more substitutes, 6-A."

We were stunned. This person in front of us was a teacher—a *permanent* teacher. He dared come into our classroom to try to replace our beloved Miss Cintron. No way. *No way!* I could practically feel the thoughts of my fellow students.

"I shall be polite and say I am pleased to make your

acquaintance, students. This is my name, a common enough one, easy to remember." The strange man turned to the board and wrote in large, neat letters, "MR. FRED."

"Your name is Mr. Fred? What's your first name, Ed?" someone asked.

"No, Ted," said someone else.

"No, Ned," added a third jokester.

"All three," I chimed in. "His name is Ed Ted Ned Fred."

The class was beginning to get over its shock. If we could demolish substitutes, we could do the same to a regular teacher.

"Ah, I see," said Mr. Fred. "The monster students are trying to make a joke. Actually, my full name is," and he wrote on the board, "GOLDBERG FRED."

"Goldberg Fred, don't you have that backward?" I asked.

"Backward? What is backward and what is forward? This is a philosophical question we might explore in the coming weeks. In the meantime, please accept as fact that my name is Goldberg Fred. Call me Mr. Fred." Mr. Fred smiled at us and opened the roll book.

"I wouldn't call him *mister* on a bet," I mumbled.

"Are you sure you're a teacher?" asked Helene.

"Are you sure you're a student?" Mr. Fred responded.

"It's Old Bad Breath getting even with us. It's a joke, isn't it?" Mike started laughing.

"Aaron Zipler." Goldberg Fred had begun reading the roll.

"Why are you calling me first? I'm last in the book," said Aaron.

"Aaron—two A's—that's first," said Goldberg Fred.

"What are you, some kind of weirdo dimbulb? Aaron is his first name. Nobody alphabetizes a roll book by first names." Crazy Arnie had always said exactly what was on his mind. He holds the school record for time spent in the principal's office.

"It's probably part of the joke," said Mike.

Goldberg Fred looked at us for a second and then continued calling names. "Alice Greenbaum. Anya Murray. Arnold Danver. Arthur Stevenson. A great many A's in this class. Interesting. Bettina Gomez."

"The man's nuts," said Arthur.

"How is he doing that?" asked Bettina. "The names in the roll book are in alphabetical order—by last name. He's calling us by first name."

"Maybe he's some kind of a genius," I said, getting worried.

"It's got to be a simple mental trick—the kind some magicians do," said Ellenbeth.

"What do you know about mental tricks?" asked Arthur.

"They explained all about them on 'ESP: Myth or Reality' last week. Didn't any of you watch it?" Ellenbeth

Maggin, my good friend, was the only kid in our class who always watched educational television. She got teased a whole lot, but secretly we all knew her television habits made her much smarter than the rest of us.

"Zarathustra Higgins. Zarathustra Higgins. Speak up, please." Goldberg Fred was looking from his roll book to the class and back again.

"There's no such person in our class," announced Alice.

"Pity," said Goldberg Fred. "Let's get to work." He turned his back on us to write on the board.

"He'll be gone in a week," said Alice, loading her blowgun. A gooey blob of paper and spit whizzed through the air. Just before it reached the back of Goldberg Fred's head, he whirled around, grabbed the flying spitball with his left hand, continued to turn, and finished writing his sentence on the board without missing a beat.

"Less than a week." Mike Carson had been folding a paper airplane and hadn't seen Goldberg Fred's move.

"This Mr. Fred is going to be a piece of cake," said Arthur, who had been watching Mike.

"A piece of cake," said Alice, reloading her blowgun.

"I hope it isn't stale," I whispered.

"What do you mean by that?" asked Alice.

"I have no idea," I said.

Sweet Reason

4

There was something about this Goldberg Fred person that wasn't normal.

I tried pointing it out to Helene, who was sitting next to me. "He's not normal," I said.

"Of course he's not normal. The man's agreed to be our permanent teacher—temporarily, of course." Helene raised her left eyebrow, a trick she had been practicing since second grade, and turned away from me.

"That's not what I mean," I said, but Helene was too busy tearing the *Weekly Reader* into confetti to pay attention to me.

My classmates hadn't noticed that Goldberg Fred had intercepted Alice's spitball without looking at it.

Was he some kind of robot with sensors buried in his greasy, long hair? While I tried to figure him out, class 6-A became fully involved in its usual teacher harassment plan. We always started slowly—a random spitball, a paper plane, a loud, rude noise, giggles—and then carefully coordinated our activities according to how the teacher was reacting. We had become a precision substitute-teacher demolition team. Goldberg Fred thought he was permanently in our classroom. We knew better. Class 6-A saw him as just another substitute standing between us and Miss Cintron. We believed we were unbeatable.

It came as quite a shock, to everyone but me, and possibly Goldberg Fred, that the morning was not going as expected. By nine forty-five, Mike had sailed ten of his best paper planes around the room. Without so much as a frown, Goldberg Fred had collected them and placed them side by side on his desktop, which was beginning to look like a miniature military airport.

"These are crude and rather primitive, Mr. Carson," said Goldberg Fred as he grabbed the last of the squadron midflight. He then took a piece of paper from a drawer and, without looking, folded it into something that sort of resembled an airplane. With a slight flick of his wrist, he launched it over our heads. It twisted and banked and flew upside down before righting itself and landing smoothly on Mike's desk.

"Aerodynamics, Mr. Carson, aerodynamics. Perhaps you would like to work on the construction of a paper helicopter. Now *that* would be an accomplishment." Goldberg Fred's arm moved in slow motion across his desk, sweeping Mike's airplanes into the wastebasket.

Mike slid down in his seat and went into a deep funk. This spurred many of my classmates into a frenzy of action. Helene began making wisecracks in her loud, foghorn voice. While we laughed, our class maniacal runners began their usual game of tag around the edge of the room. Crazy Arnie climbed onto a table and sang his medley of top-ten hits from the 1950s. A couple of kids took comic books from their desks and began reading. Helene tossed her confetti at the runners each time they passed her desk. Even Bettina, who usually sat quietly while we worked on substitutes, joined Ellenbeth in a game of desktop jacks.

I looked around the room, and the awful truth sank in. We had been with weird Goldberg Fred, the piece of cake, for less than an hour, and we had already used up almost a week's worth of "drive the teacher crazy" tricks. While class 6-A went bananas, Goldberg Fred sat calmly on the edge of his desk. The only parts of him that moved were his eyes and one snakelike arm as he batted the spitballs away from his peaceful, happy face.

"Anya, why are you just sitting there? Do something," Helene demanded.

"Like what?" I asked.

"Like anything. Stand on your head. Make awful noises. Join the runners. Anything."

"What for?" I asked.

"To make this geep go away."

I looked at Goldberg Fred, who moved to the teacher's chair, put his feet on the desk, and closed his eyes.

"I think he's taking a nap," I said.

"He can't be sleeping; he's still picking Alice's spitballs out of the air," said Helene.

"His eyes are closed," I said.

"It's just another mental trick," said Ellenbeth, bouncing her jack ball off the ceiling.

"TAKE A BREAK, ALICE," I shouted across the room. Alice's face had turned bright red, and she looked as if she might faint.

"I have to get him at least once!" Alice gasped as she took a new straw from her desk.

The class had gone beyond chaos. I stood up. It was time for me to act like a president. "EVERYONE STOP!" I yelled. As usual, nobody listened. In fact, things seemed to get worse. It was getting dangerous in the room. Someone was going to get hurt. I tried shouting again, with the same results. Goldberg Fred didn't move. The stupid, happy smile was still on his face. Maybe he was waiting for a few kids to crash into each other—to reduce our numbers. That was it, a diabolical plan. Pomeroy had to be in on it. The revenge of the teachers. Let class 6-A self-destruct.

I decided to risk my own life and reputation for the sake of our cause and public safety. After all, I *was* president. A leader should lead. If my mother wanted a mensch, she'd have a mensch. I ran to the door, opened it, and shouted, "HELLO MISS CINTRON, YOU'RE BACK! HOW WONDERFUL . . ."

Everyone froze in place. Mouths hung open in mid-shouts. Arms stopped halfway through throws. Runners stopped midstride. I could almost swear a spitball hung in the air just in front of Alice's blowgun. I closed the door quietly.

"Let her in, Anya."

"Don't lock her out. Let her in."

"She's back."

My classmates were so happy and relieved, a number of eyes filled with tears. I took a deep breath, kept my hand on the doorknob in case I had to get out fast, and spoke. "Miss Cintron isn't really here. You were out of control. You were going to get hurt. I had to trick you. I'm sorry. I have something important to tell you." I dove for cover just after the first heavy missile skimmed by my head. Cover turned out to be behind Goldberg Fred's desk. I don't know why I didn't leave the room the way I had planned.

"TRAITOR!" "FINK!" "NERD!" "ROMULON!"

"Romulon?" asked Goldberg Fred, sitting down next to me on the floor.

"The worst kind of traitor a person can be," I explained.

"Ah, I see. A Romulon is to TV brains what Quisling is to the rest of us," said Goldberg Fred.

"What's a quisling?" I asked.

"Who and what. Vidkun Quisling was a Norwegian traitor in World War Two. His name has become a word meaning 'traitor.' If I call you a quisling, I am calling you a traitor."

"What happened to Quisling—the man not the word?"

"He was executed." Goldberg Fred smiled at me.

I gave him my dirtiest look and stood up. I turned my back to my raving classmates, picked up a piece of chalk, and began writing on the board:

WE HAVE BEEN TRICKED BY OLD BAD BREATH.
HE WANTS US TO RIOT. THIS WAS ALL PLANNED.
STOP NOW. I'LL EXPLANE.

"It's E-X-P-L-A-I-N. You spelled it wrong," Bettina shouted.

"Thanks," I said, correcting my mistake.

"Start explaining."

"Yeah, explain!"

"Where's that Fred guy?"

I pointed behind the desk. Out of sight of the class, Goldberg Fred was sitting crosslegged on the floor, tightening the screws on the bottom of his chair and dabbing them with Crazy Glue.

"Hiding, huh? Chalk up another one for class 6-A, Alice. Write it in the log. Hear that Mike? You can cheer up now." Arthur leaned over and gave Mike a friendly poke in the arm.

"He's not hiding; he's gluing the screws on the chair," I said.

"Why?" asked Ellenbeth.

"Probably so we won't be able to loosen them and make the chair collapse the way we did with substitute number three," said Mike, putting his head down on his desk.

"An accurate deduction. You might have some latent talent for scientific endeavors after all, Mr. Carson." Goldberg Fred stood up and glanced at the board.

"Practicing to be a writer of fiction, Miss Murray?"

"It's not fiction." I turned to my friends. "He's a plant. A spy. A trick. Pomeroy brought him here to break us. Old Bad Breath wants to get even with us for what we did to the other teachers. He told this so-called Goldberg Fred exactly what we do to teachers. He prepared him. Haven't you noticed that nothing we do bothers him? We're supposed to get all worked up, get ourselves into trouble, and maybe even hurt so we get expelled or land in a hospital. Can't you tell that this guy isn't really a teacher? What teacher dresses that way? What teacher lets a bunch of kids run around the room at top speed for an hour?"

"So what is he, Anya?"

"Yeah, what is he, a Martian?"

"Mars is uninhabitable," said Goldberg Fred.

"See what I mean?" I said to my friends. "What teacher gets called a name and answers with a fact?"

"A good one, I would think," said Goldberg Fred. "Besides, I don't consider 'Martian' to be a fighting word. Now sit down, Miss Murray. The runners may stay collapsed on the floor where they are. Miss Greenbaum, I think you would have far more success with your spitball blowgun if you patterned it after those actually used in some of the less technically advanced parts of the world. You may research the design in the public library—on your own time.

"As for Miss Murray's speculations, what does it matter what I am or why I was hired? I am here to stay. Miss Cintron is not coming back until next year. That is a fact. Accept it." Goldberg Fred looked at the wall clock. "We have exactly one hour and ten minutes until lunch. I challenge you. In that time, if you can aggravate me, annoy me, make me sick of you, or even give me a slight headache, I will resign, leaving you to the mercy of Mr. Pomeroy and what I deduce is your dubious plan to force Miss Cintron to return."

"And if we can't do any of those things?" I asked.

"You are mine for the rest of the year." Goldberg Fred closed his eyes and chuckled. "You may discuss this amongst yourselves if you wish."

The class crowded together in the back of the room. "I don't like this, Anya. The man is strange," said Ellenbeth.

"I thought you said he was using simple mental tricks," said Aaron.

"So what if I did. He gives me the willies." Ellenbeth shivered.

"What're the willies?" asked Arthur.

"The creepy crawlies, the weirds, the—" Crazy Arnold began.

"But he's just a nerdish nebbish. He's harmless," Helene insisted.

"He's getting to you," I said.

"All of you are overreacting," Helene said.

"What do you mean by 'all of *you*'?" I asked.

"Okay, okay. *We're* on the brink of hysteria because that extremely strange man just sits there and smiles."

"With his eyes closed," Alice added.

"I don't think he's human," said Paul Saladino.

"Be real. You never think anyone who gives you trouble is human," Arthur complained.

"Someday I'm going to be right."

"Stick to the point. Do we accept his challenge?" I asked.

"If we lose, he stays."

"How can we lose?"

"Nothing's bothered him yet."

"We haven't tried high-pitched screaming."

"That gives *me* a headache."

"How do we know if we've given him a headache? He's not going to admit it."

"I can always tell when I give an adult a headache—the eyes go funny and the forehead usually wrinkles."

"We'll have to do more than make noise. We have to be disgusting, too."

"How?"

"You don't want an explanation."

"Do we fight for Miss Cintron's return?"

"Let's get to it!"

We turned to Goldberg Fred. "We're ready."

He leaned his chair against the chalkboard, put his hands behind his head, his feet on the desk, the stupid smile on his face, and closed his eyes. "Go to it. Give it your best shot, kiddies."

And we did. We were loud. We were disgusting. We

were insulting. We were obnoxious. At noon, our deadline, we were also exhausted.

"I shall introduce you to the genius of John Philip Sousa as we go to lunch." Goldberg Fred lined us up, grabbed a portable tape player from his desk, and, arms swinging to the music—like a drum major in a parade—marched us to the cafeteria.

"Feeling better?" he asked as we rounded the last corner and lined up behind 6-C. Slumping against each other for support, nobody answered him. We were too tired and confused and hungry to talk much during lunch.

"They're not throwing their food or making retching noises or harassing the other students. How did you do it?" Old Bad Breath had come over to our table.

"By the use of sweet reason, Mr. Pomeroy," said Goldberg Fred, taking a last spoonful of chocolate pudding before reaching for his hot turkey sandwich.

Taking the Test

5

After lunch and recess, Goldberg Fred seemed to forget we were in the room. Turning up his tape player to full volume, he began cleaning the mess we had made in the morning. One by one we began to help. I couldn't understand why, but instead of thinking about a foolproof way to get rid of the man, I found myself working alongside my friends. We swept up confetti, righted desks, washed paint off walls, straightened rows of books. As soon as the Sousa tape ran out, Goldberg Fred would begin it again.

There was something about the music that made us happy, even when we would have preferred to be miserable. By the third time through, kids were humming along, making noises like trombones, trumpets, and drums as they worked. I am a stubborn person—I tried holding out, but each time I stopped concentrating, my foot began tapping out the rhythms of the marches. Cleaning became fun. By two o'clock, the room looked as neat as it had when Miss Cintron had been around— maybe even a little bit neater. I felt like a traitor.

"Very nice," said Goldberg Fred. "Now for the test."

"Test?"

"What test?"

"You haven't taught us anything yet."

"So you say," said Goldberg Fred, handing out paper.

"Of course we say so." I stood up. "And as class president . . . ," I began.

"Sit down, Miss Murray. Teachers outrank presidents."

"Says who?" I expected my classmates to back me up with smart remarks and their usual rude noises, but they sort of took a deep breath and held it. I was on my own.

"I say," said Goldberg Fred.

"All presidents? Do you think teachers outrank *all* presidents?" I grinned a triumphant grin and winked at the class. They appeared to be still holding their breaths.

"As a matter of fact, in importance, yes." Goldberg Fred turned to the chalkboard and began writing.

I took one final look around the room. "You can breathe now—you quislings." I sat down.

"What did you call us?" demanded Kathy.

"Look it up," I snapped.

"Pencil or pen will be just fine. Begin writing as soon as you're ready. There will be only five questions on this test." Goldberg Fred giggled as he continued to write.

"He's pretty creepy," whispered Aaron.

"What did he mean about teachers and presidents, Anya?" asked Bettina.

"Why ask me?"

"Because you're a president."

"Big deal. Where were you when I needed you?"

"I couldn't say anything," said Bettina.

"What do you mean?" I asked.

"I just couldn't talk." Bettina looked worried.

"Why?" I demanded.

"I don't know."

"I couldn't say anything either," said Paul.

"Me either."

"Me either." Whispers came from around the room.

"Only forty-five minutes left," Goldberg Fred announced.

The class studied the board and began writing.

These were Goldberg Fred's test questions:

1. WHY DO YOU, PERSONALLY, COME TO SCHOOL EVERY DAY?

2. IF YOU DIDN'T COME TO SCHOOL, WHAT
WOULD YOU DO WITH YOUR TIME?

3. IF YOU COULD GO ANYWHERE IN THE WORLD,
OR OUT OF IT, WHERE WOULD IT BE? WHY?

4. IF YOU COULD BE ANYTHING IN THE WORLD,
WHAT WOULD YOU BE? WHY?

5. IF YOU HAD A CHOICE BETWEEN MISS CIN-
TRON COMING BACK TO SCHOOL TO PLEASE YOU
OR STAYING IN SOUTH AMERICA TO DO WHAT
SHE HAS ALWAYS WANTED TO DO, WHICH WOULD
YOU CHOOSE? WHY?

"What kind of test is this? You don't have to know anything," complained Ellenbeth.

"On the contrary, you have to know yourselves." Goldberg Fred started bobbing around the room like a big turkey, looking out the windows, examining books on the shelves, measuring the walls, studying the ceiling as if something were up there.

"You're making me nervous," said Alice.

"Does that mean I can expect a blowgun attack on my person?" asked Goldberg Fred.

"Not right now," said Alice, rolling a straw back and forth between two fingers.

"The last question is a trick." Crazy Arnie slammed his hand down on his desk.

"How so?" asked Goldberg Fred.

"You're on the last question already?" Ellenbeth, the class brain, sounded annoyed.

"I always start with the last question. It makes me feel better if I don't finish the whole test."

"Good boy," said Goldberg Fred.

Crazy Arnie looked at Goldberg Fred suspiciously. "Anyway, question five is a trick."

"Matters of conscience are always difficult," said Goldberg Fred. "No more talking. You have thirty minutes left before the bell."

At three o'clock Goldberg Fred collected our papers.

"It's been a pleasure besting you, 6-A." Goldberg Fred opened the door and led us to freedom.

"What a crock," I complained to Arthur and Helene on the way home.

"I don't know. Those were interesting questions— especially the last one." Helene moved so Arthur was between us. "I think Miss Cintron has a right to do what she wants with her life without our trying to mess it up and force her to come home. It's our own fault that we're going to be stuck with Goldberg Fred, weirdo of the universe. We chased everyone else away."

"Are you afraid I'm going to hit you or something, Helene?" I asked as Helene inched over to the edge of the sidewalk.

"Do you think your mother'll mind my coming over for dinner?"

"Don't change the subject."

"Yes."

"Yes you think I'd hit you? That's rotten."

"Well, you really wanted your plan to work and it didn't. You're pretty mad. And you have been known to throw a punch."

"When I was a little kid."

"Like last year?"

"That was an arm punch. He deserved it."

"A punch is a punch."

"No it isn't. Besides, you're my best friend. I would never hit you. Anyway, I'm too mature now to use physical violence to win an argument."

"Good, because I think we've definitely lost the battle with Mr. Fred."

"You're wrong. My plan hasn't failed yet. It's only been one day with Goldberg Fred."

"Maybe it *should* fail," said Arthur.

"What? Are you nuts?" I slapped Arthur on the arm.

"You said you weren't going to hit," he complained.

"That was Helene, not you."

"So much for maturity," Helene mumbled.

"Mr. Fred isn't that bad." Arthur jumped away from me as he spoke.

"Right, and hot lava is good to swim in. Look, Arthur,

the man is strange. Start with his clothing—the stupid jacket and tie."

"And the shoes and the pants—and how about the red socks?" Helene was starting to giggle.

"You can laugh now, but how did you feel walking into the cafeteria with the all-time champion nerd teacher?" I asked.

"Nobody blames us for how he looks—or walks— unless they think we dress him in the morning when we take him out of the closet. Mr. Fred, robot teacher." Arthur began laughing.

"It's NOT FUNNY," I shouted. "I can't stand it. Can't you see that the man is a slick, tricky slime who has been hired by that rat Old Bad Breath to get us."

"Is he a nerd or a slick slime? He can't be both, Anya," said Helene.

"Yes he can, because he is."

"Did you notice that he didn't get hit by one spitball?" asked Arthur. "How did he do that?"

"It was more than good hand-eye coordination," I said. "His back was to Alice when she shot at him the first time. And how about the paper airplanes?"

"What about them?" asked Arthur.

"His planes flew like someone was piloting them."

"He said it was aerodynamics," explained Arthur.

"And you believed him?"

"I didn't think about it, Anya."

"You should have."

"You know what some of the kids are saying?" asked Helene.

"What?" I asked.

"That it's your fault we're stuck with him."

"My fault? How?"

"If you hadn't stopped us when we were really going good this morning, we would have driven him away like the others."

"THE MAN WAS SLEEPING, FOR CRYING OUT LOUD!" I screamed. "HE COULDN'T HAVE CARED LESS IF WE WERE SWINGING FROM THE CEILING OR THROWING OURSELVES OUT WINDOWS!"

"You don't have to shout at me. I didn't say it," said Helene.

"Why didn't anyone help me this afternoon—especially you two?"

"When?" Helene asked innocently.

"You know when. When you all left me standing there alone—no support—no backup."

"Oh, you mean that thing about presidents and teachers?" said Arthur.

"Yeah, that thing. Everyone said they couldn't talk. Sounded like an attack of serious chicken to me," I said.

"But we *couldn't* speak," said Helene.

"Or make noises," said Arthur.

"Really *couldn't* or wouldn't?" I asked.

"Couldn't, Anya, *couldn't*." Helene stopped and stared at me.

"Don't you think that's very strange?" I asked my friends.

"Ellenbeth said it must have been mass hysteria or mind control," said Helene.

"Ellenbeth says a whole lot of things. We weren't hysterical—at least not right then," I said.

"That leaves mind control," said Arthur.

"And about a million other things," I insisted.

"Like what?" asked Helene.

"My mom likes having you over for dinner," I said.

"You changed the subject."

"I know."

Mr. Fred, the Butterfly

6

Helene and I hung around together for the rest of the afternoon. When my mother got home, she was in a very good mood. The school secretary had called her at work to say that the problem with 6-A had been solved by a new teacher, and no parent-principal meeting would be necessary. In celebration, my mother decided to make salad and spaghetti instead of microwaving our usual Monday-night frozen dinners.

"What's the name of your new teacher?" asked my mother, as she filled our bowls with spaghetti. My mother always serves spaghetti in bowls, so the meatballs won't escape— when we have meatballs, which we didn't that night.

"He's not *my* teacher. I hate him," I grumped.

"Nevertheless, he must have a name." My mother sounded disgustingly cheerful.

"Fred," said Helene.

"You call your new teacher by his first name? How informal. I'm not sure I approve."

"No, Mrs. Murray. His last name is Fred. Mr. Fred. Mr. Goldberg Fred." Helene winked at me.

"You must have misunderstood him, Helene, dear. Goldberg is a last name. His name must be Fred Goldberg."

"No, Mom. We're not idiots. We're sixth graders. We asked him and he was very clear. He wrote it on the board. His name is Goldberg Fred—Mr. Fred—and he's the weirdest person alive. I hate him."

"That's a bit strong. Dislike, perhaps. Not appreciate, maybe. But hate? How can you possibly hate a person you hardly know?"

"I hate him. His name is backward. He was wearing a plaid jacket with checked trousers. . . ."

"Don't forget the bow tie, the red socks, and the blue suede shoes," Helene interrupted.

"Who could forget them?"

"How horrible. The man does not dress fashionably." My mother shook her head in make-believe sympathy. She was not taking us seriously.

"Well, he also eats chocolate pudding *before* he eats his lunch."

"Sounds like a terrible monster to me." Now my mother was actually laughing.

"What's the use? You'll never understand," I complained.

"I understand that this Goldberg Fred is the first teacher in weeks to get class 6-A under control. He can't be all bad."

"Yeah, well he told Alice how to make a better blowgun. What do you think of a teacher who does that?"

"Alice takes a blowgun to school?"

"It's just a straw that shoots spitballs, Mrs. Murray. And Mr. Fred didn't exactly give Alice instructions." Helene smiled winningly at my mother.

"Just a straw that shoots spitballs? In school? It's a miracle any teacher at all is willing to step in front of you monsters."

"Mother!"

"What would *you* call a class of children who take pleasure in torturing hardworking teachers? Angels?" We finished our food in silence.

"Why don't you go get the dessert, Anya." My mother stacked our empty bowls and handed them to Helene, who followed me into the kitchen.

"How could you take his side, Helene?"

"I didn't."

"You said Goldberg Fred didn't give Alice blowgun instructions."

"He didn't. He told her to look them up in the library."

"It's the same thing."

"Isn't."

"Is."

"Where's the dessert, girls?" My mother called from the other room.

When we had finished our ice-cream bars, my mother announced, "I'd like to meet this Mr. Fred of yours. I think it's going to be a good school year after all."

"He's not *my* Mr. Fred, and you'd hate him," I insisted.

Tuesday morning was a rainy, gloomy, cold, October day—perfect for my mood. I slogged through the puddles and refused to say a word to Arthur.

Halfway to school Arthur called me a grouch and walked ahead to join some happier people.

"You're a potato brain, Arthur." Arthur ignored my insult, which, of course, made me grouchier.

Before school each day at My Dear Watson, students line up in the playground or, when the weather is bad, in the gym. Tuesday was a gym day. Without looking at the soggy crowd, I pulled off my boots and rain slicker, shook them a couple of times over the rubber mat, and dragged myself over to 6-A's corner.

The first person I noticed was Alice, who was carrying a long cardboard tube wrapped in plastic.

"What's that?"

"My new blowgun case."

"How many do you have in there?" I asked, looking at the long, fat tube and thinking of straws.

"Just one. I went to the library and did research. Then I went home and made this. It's bamboo." Alice let me peek into the end of the tube.

"It's an awfully fat blowgun, Alice. It's going to take a spitball the size of a marble." I was impressed.

"Oh, this isn't for spitballs. This blowgun shoots darts. Poison darts." Alice had a strange gleam in her eye.

I backed away from her. It was sometimes hard to tell if Alice was making a joke or being serious. I didn't want to be involved in murder—or become her practice target. I looked around for the doomed Goldberg Fred. He was nowhere in sight.

"Where's Goldberg Fred?" I asked no one in particular.

"Hasn't shown up yet," said Aaron. "Maybe his parts rusted in the rain."

"What parts?"

"His robot parts. Arthur says Fred probably isn't human."

"Then it would be his android parts," said Susan Ames. "A humanlike robot is an android, and android parts don't rust."

"How do *you* know?" Aaron was ready for an argument, but the bell rang and interrupted him.

"Anya, should we go upstairs without a teacher?" Kathy asked.

"Why ask me?"

"You're the president."

"We'll vote," I said. "All in favor of going to our room, say 'room.'" Everyone said "room."

We trudged up the stairs to the attic of our old building. It was well-known that 6-A was the best classroom in the school. It had giant windows, a skylight, lots of floor space, and an attached smaller room with sinks and tables. That day, I think we all would have traded it for a regular, dull classroom, with tiny windows that didn't open—or a broom closet with no windows at all—if we could have had Miss Cintron as our teacher again.

"Maybe I was wrong and you were right, Anya. Maybe Mr. Fred gave up after all," said Helene hopefully.

"He's probably waiting to ambush us on the top landing."

I stared at the floor as I shuffled through the main classroom to the little hallway that served as our closet. The door leading from it to the smaller back room was shut. I hung my slicker and hat on my hook and went to my desk. I wanted everyone to know how miserable I was. Maybe some of them would feel guilty about say-

55
*

ing rotten things about me. I am a very good sulker. I slumped in my seat and stared at my hands which I folded on my desk. After a few minutes, I put my head on my arms. I waited for the sympathy. I waited for someone to notice.

Nobody did. I realized that my classmates were making strange noises like, "ahhhhh" and "oooo" and "geeee." They were not saying "poor Anya" or even "what's wrong with Anya?" What was wrong with them?

I looked up. "Holy cow!" I blurted. One entire wall was covered with maps and photographs. There were maps of the world, maps of countries, maps of cities, and black-and-white maps of the universe. There were treasure maps and old-fashioned-looking navigation charts decorated with drawings of sailing ships and whales. Around the maps hung pictures of mountains, oceans, castles, underground caves, sunken ships, strange rocks, deserts, and people of every size, shape, color, and costume.

I turned to the back wall of the room which, since Miss Cintron left, had been empty. It had been made into an enormous bulletin board. Two-foot-high letters spelled out the word "THINK." I noticed that many of my friends were staring at the ceiling. I half expected to see Goldberg Fred hanging from his feet like a bat. Instead, hanging from string cut into different lengths were models of planes and spaceships, birds, butterflies, bees, and dragonflies. They darted and swayed and dipped over our heads.

"How are they moving?" asked Arthur.

"Look." Ellenbeth pointed to a small fan mounted in a corner of the ceiling.

"He must have been here all night."

"Those are beautiful. Do you think he made them?"

"Look at that dragonfly—it's put together like a biplane."

"Probably it was the other way around. Humans have adapted many designs from nature." A man's voice brought our attention to the front of the room. The whole class was surprised to see him there. He must have walked in after us.

"Did you do this?" I asked, waving toward the ceiling and the walls.

"Yes," said the man, opening a roll book. He was tall with curly black hair and a large mustache. He wore gold-rimmed glasses, a denim shirt without a tie, worn jeans, and hiking boots. He looked familiar, but I couldn't quite place him.

"What happened to Mr. Fred?" asked Alice, unwrapping her blowgun. She looked disappointed. I was sitting too far from her to tell if she had a bagful of darts.

"Nothing," said the man, laughing.

"Well, what's so funny, and who are you anyway?" I demanded.

The man smiled and I recognized him. "ANOTHER TRICK!" I shouted. "THAT MAN IS AN IMPOSTER! A FAKE!"

"What are you talking about, Anya?" asked Ellenbeth.

"HIM! He's not who he is. He's Goldberg Fred, the weirdo."

"He couldn't be; he's cute," said Kathy.

"You're nuts, Anya," said Aaron.

"I don't think so. Look at him closely," said Helene.

As if to help in the identification, the man in the front of the room hunched over slightly, walked in little circles, bobbed his head and twisted his long fingers together.

"For once Miss Murray is correct. Goldberg Fred, the weirdo, and I are one and the same," said the man.

"And exactly who or what *are* you?" asked Alice, lowering her three-foot-long blowgun.

"I am Goldberg Fred, your teacher, and you'll be delighted to know that all of you passed yesterday's test."

"Slimy trickster," I mumbled to myself.

"Kathy's right; he's kind of cute," someone whispered from the back of the room.

"It's like a caterpillar turning into a butterfly," someone else added.

"A bug is what he is all right," I said.

Goldberg Fred winked at me, peeled off his mustache, and stuck it to the chalkboard. He looked at the roll book. "Aaron Zipler," he said.

Slimy Goldberg Fred

7

elda Zabar." Goldberg Fred looked around the room.

"Why do you do that?" asked Ellenbeth.

"Do what, Miss Maggin?"

"Make up a name at the end of roll call."

"Are you saying that there is no Zelda Zabar in this class?" asked Goldberg Fred.

"No," began Ellenbeth. "What I'm saying is—"

"Ah, then there *is* a Zelda Zabar in this class," interrupted Goldberg Fred.

"No there isn't, but—" Ellenbeth began again.

"Pity," said Goldberg Fred and handed Ellenbeth a

pile of papers. "Please pass these out, Miss Maggin. They are yesterday's exams."

"Hey, you left off my grade," Kathy Pepper complained.

"No one got a grade," said Ellenbeth.

"I corrected spelling and grammar errors. Everyone passed the test." Goldberg Fred sat down on the edge of his desk.

"But how did we do?" Kathy insisted.

"You each presumably did the best you could. Isn't it enough to know that?" Goldberg Fred took a pen from his pocket.

"Does that mean I got an A?" Kathy said.

"Do you think you earned an A?" asked Goldberg Fred.

"I'm an A student," Kathy insisted. "I want my grade."

"Why?"

"Because."

"This test wasn't a competition, Miss Pepper."

"In school you get grades," Kathy whined.

"Why?"

"What do you mean, *why?*" asked Kathy. "You're a teacher."

"What do you mean by *why,* Miss Pepper? You're a student."

"This is confusing me," someone whispered.

"I think it's funny," said Helene.

"I demand you give me a grade on this test," said Kathy.

"I'd leave it alone if I were you, Kath," I warned.

"Keep out of this, Anya. You're president, not queen. You don't know everything. Grades are important. Now, where is my grade?" Kathy shoved her paper at Goldberg Fred, who took it from her hand.

"Well, if you insist." Goldberg Fred wrote on the paper, and handed it to Kathy.

"Hey! Hey! You can't do this to me!" Kathy shouted.

"Is something wrong, Miss Pepper?" asked Goldberg Fred.

"I warned you," I whispered. He is so slimy, I thought to myself.

"You did, indeed, warn your friend, Miss Murray. Your suspicions about me are almost on the mark. I am tricky, underhanded, and devious. I will do almost anything to encourage learning—and that includes on-the-spot floggings, minor tortures, and executions when necessary. The one thing I am not is slimy, so stop thinking of me in that way. Understood?"

"How did you know what I was thinking?" The man was starting to frighten me.

"I have extremely good hearing," said Goldberg Fred.

"He's got to be joking about the executions," said Helene.

"And the torture . . ."

"And the floggings . . ."

"I don't think so! Look what he did to my test. *My* test." Kathy held it up so we could all see the enormous red C written right in the middle of the page.

"So what's the big deal?" asked Arthur, who didn't know there was another grade a person could get.

"I've never gotten less than a B + in my life." Kathy was almost crying.

"You forced him to grade it. It's your own fault." Ellenbeth shoved her test paper into her desk. "He's not getting his hands on mine."

"Why should a grade upset you, Miss Pepper? If you don't like it, change it." Goldberg Fred went to the chalkboard.

"CHANGE IT?" shouted Kathy. "THAT'S ILLEGAL!"

"Do you think the grade police will come and get you? This is a classroom, not the real world," Goldberg Fred said over his shoulder.

"IT'S WRONG TO CHANGE A GRADE!" Kathy was still shouting. "IF YOU DON'T BELIEVE ME, ASK MR. POMEROY. WHAT KIND OF TEACHER ARE YOU ANYWAY?" Kathy had lost it. She was standing in the aisle, stomping her feet, and breathing hard.

"Maybe we should call the school nurse," Mike suggested.

"Not necessary." Goldberg Fred had finished writing on the board. He turned to face the furious Kathy. "Miss

Pepper, you are making a jackass of yourself," he said calmly.

Kathy stuttered, "You you you . . ." Then her mouth snapped shut.

"I think the word should be *jennyass* since Kathy is female," Ellenbeth mused.

"You may be right. Please look it up." Goldberg Fred turned back to Kathy. "Please sit down, Miss Pepper. We should begin the day's work. If we continue at this pace, we'll never finish in time." Goldberg Fred picked up Alice's blowgun.

"In time for what?" someone asked.

"None of your business," said Goldberg Fred, closing one eye and peering down the blowgun with the other.

I looked around the room. Goldberg Fred had the absolute attention of everyone. It was a good time to try something out. Goldberg Fred is a slimy, rat-eating snake of a teacher who will never hear the word *mister* spoken by this student, I thought to myself.

"Snakes are not slimy, Miss Murray, and neither am I—and nothing in the rules requires you to use the title *mister* before my name until you feel I have earned your respect." Goldberg Fred continued to examine the blowgun.

"What did he mean by that?" asked Helene.

"You wouldn't believe me," I said.

"No, they wouldn't," said Goldberg Fred. "Alice, this

is a decent weapon—perhaps a bit shorter than regulation, and not carved or decorated, but nice and straight and effective. Have you ever thought of constructing a more complicated implement of death?"

"Is he telling Alice to make a better weapon?" Louise's horrified voice squeaked. We all knew that Alice had no fear of aiming at anyone—anytime. We had all had her disgusting spitballs stuck to us. And it wasn't a matter of Alice being angry or even annoyed. Alice whizzed spitballs through the air when she was bored, happy, or sad. It was something she liked to do.

"She's already made a better weapon. That blowgun throws darts," I said, wondering if Alice had tipped her darts with a fast-acting or slow-acting poison. Would I have time for some good last words?

"Did she bring any darts to school?" Helene ducked under her desk and waited for an answer. We all laughed nervously.

"This, the first concrete example that a member of class 6-A is capable of doing independent, creative work based on solid research, will hang on the back wall from this day forward." Goldberg Fred placed the blowgun on his desk.

"I want my blowgun back," said Alice.

"I may be eccentric, Alice, but I'm not crazy. No weapons are allowed in this classroom—in student hands." Goldberg Fred turned to the chalkboard.

"Why are you calling me Alice?"

"That's your name, isn't it?" Goldberg Fred finished writing, put down the chalk, wiped his hands on his jeans, and turned to face us.

"But you call everyone else by their last names," said Alice.

"So?"

"So why call *me* Alice?"

"*Because* that's your name."

Alice made a strangled sound and put her head on her desk.

"Two down, twenty-three to go," someone whispered.

"I think I hate that man," someone else whispered.

Twenty-five heads nodded in agreement, but not a single one dared take its eyes off the terrible, tricky, mean, evil, and slimy Goldberg Fred.

Two Ears, One Mouth, and a Foot

8

W hat does that mean?" asked Arthur, pointing to the board. Goldberg Fred had written:

NATURE HAS GIVEN US TWO EARS BUT ONLY ONE MOUTH.
(Benjamin Disraeli: 1804–1881)

Goldberg Fred looked at Arthur and added:

A CLOSED MOUTH GATHERS NO FEET.

"Oh," said Arthur.
"Oh?" asked Kathy. "You understand the second sentence but not the first?"

"No. Now I understand both," said Arthur.

"Who is Benjamin Dis-Dis—" began Aaron.

"Diz-rail-ee," Ellenbeth pronounced clearly and slowly.

"Was he on public television, too?" asked Aaron. A few kids giggled.

"He's been dead for over a hundred years," said Ellenbeth. "Look at the dates."

"You know what I mean," Aaron said.

"The problem is that *you* don't know what you mean. Of course, if you watched PBS, you wouldn't be so ignorant." Ellenbeth was on the attack.

"Here comes the lecture," said Helene. None of us minded Ellenbeth knowing more than we did. In fact, since third grade, she had been saving most of us a whole lot of time. We all had Ellenbeth's phone number memorized for homework emergencies, or general information questions. Much of the time Ellenbeth was just as good as the junior encyclopedia.

Ellenbeth ignored Helene's comment and launched into her speech. We settled into our seats. Ellenbeth was pretty interesting most of the time. "It just so happens that Benjamin Disraeli was a great man. Even though he wasn't in power very long, under his influence, the poor people of England really benefited. In case you didn't know, Disraeli was—"

Goldberg Fred squeaked the chalk across the board a

couple of times, interrupting Ellenbeth and stopping all thought in the room for a few seconds.

"Ouch!" Kids clamped their hands over their ears and made horrible faces.

Goldberg Fred wrote:

KNOWLEDGE IS LIKE A GARDEN: IF IT IS NOT CULTIVATED, IT CANNOT BE HARVESTED.

"Do some research about him yourself, Mr. Zipler." Goldberg Fred tossed the chalk from hand to hand.

"About who?" Aaron asked.

"Actually, *anyone* interesting will do."

"How will I know who's interesting before I look them up?" Aaron turned and winked at the class.

"Him or her up," said Goldberg Fred.

"What?" said Aaron.

"*Who's interesting* is singular. *Them* is plural."

"What?" said Aaron.

"Actually, you have posed your first intellectual conundrum. If given no specific assignment or clues, how do you know which people to study before you actually study them? And from this crowd of unknown, interesting people, how do you pick one?"

"What's a conundrum?" asked Aaron.

"Look it up," said Goldberg Fred as he wrote:

HE WHO DOES NOT CULTIVATE HIS OWN FIELD
WILL DIE OF HUNGER!

Helene started laughing.

"Stop it, Helene," I ordered.

"No," she said. "This Fred guy is very good—and funny. I admire humor."

"You're warped."

"He's mean as a snake," said Kathy.

"A smart, very fast snake," Helene giggled.

"Snakes don't have thoughts or emotions," said Ellenbeth. "They can't be mean or nice or," she looked at Helene, "smart."

Helene smiled and raised an eyebrow at Ellenbeth, but before Helene could speak, Ellenbeth added, ". . . or funny."

Kathy was looking for an excuse to argue. "How do you know so much about snakes, Miss Encyclopedia Mouth?" Kathy sneered. "You probably have snakes as close relatives."

"At least *I've* never gotten a C. And it's *Ms.* Encyclopedia Mouth to you," Ellenbeth answered.

Kathy began to get out of her seat.

"FIGHT! FIGHT! There's going to be a fight!" Crazy Arnie stood up on his chair and began waving his arms wildly.

"Did you notice that Ellenbeth made a joke?" Helene raised her voice over the din.

"Have you noticed that 'very good, funny Fred' has started a riot?" I answered.

"How?" asked Helene.

"By giving Kathy a C and turning her into a wild woman."

"She asked for it," said Helene.

"I heard that," said Kathy, turning to Helene.

"SAVED BY THE CLASS MOUTH," shouted Crazy Arnie. Then, the strangest thing happened. He stepped off his chair, walked up to the board, took a piece of chalk and wrote:

HE WHO LEARNS, TEACHES.

"Why did you write that?" I asked.

"I felt like it?" said Crazy Arnie, looking puzzled.

"What does it mean?" asked Bettina.

Crazy Arnie shook his head and returned to his seat.

"Too weird," said Paul.

"Curiouser and curiouser," giggled Helene.

"I do *not* understand why you feel all of this is so funny," I whispered to Helene.

"It's impossible to explain humor. You either get it or you don't," she said.

"In this case, I don't."

"I know. Too bad."

The fight was forgotten. Goldberg Fred settled himself behind his desk and began sorting through the drawers. He placed a yo-yo, three whistles, one whoopee cushion, a bag of marbles, a pile of jacks, some tennis balls, a pink spalding, a bunch of deflated balloons, and a large quantity of bubble gum—unchewed, on the desktop. It was some of the stuff taken from us by substitute teachers.

"Come and get it," said Goldberg Fred, removing a drawer and dumping its contents on top of the things already on the desk.

"Is this a trick, Anya?" someone whispered.

"Probably," I said. "He wants to find out who brought in that stuff."

"We *all* brought in something," said Alice, eyeing an unopened box of straws.

Goldberg Fred reached into the pile and grabbed the spalding. "Here's your ball, Mr. Stevenson." He tossed it to Arthur. "And yours, Miss Gomez, and yours, Mr. Saladino." Goldberg Fred threw two tennis balls to Bettina and one to Paul.

"How does he know?" asked Bettina.

Goldberg Fred lifted the wastebasket so its top was level with the top of the desk. "Retrieve these teacher-torture devices or forfeit them. You have two minutes."

No one moved—until we heard the metallic clunk of a jack bouncing on the bottom of the empty basket.

In less than two minutes, the desktop was clear.

Goldberg Fred yawned. He stretched, folded his arms across his chest, and closed his eyes. We watched him and waited.

"What's happening?" someone whispered.

"Nothing," someone else whispered.

"Why are you whispering?" I asked.

"Shhhhh," said someone.

The only sounds in the room were Goldberg Fred's snores and the clock as the hand jumped from one minute marker to the next.

"It's been three minutes," said Alice, writing in the log.

"Shhhhh," said someone.

"Stop that!" I stood up.

"Stop what?" someone whispered.

"Stop shushing and whispering."

"But Mr. Fred's asleep," whispered Susan.

"So what!" I said. "He's supposed to be awake so we can get rid of him."

"Why, Anya?" Helene asked.

"What do you mean 'why'? It's our plan. You know, the one to get Miss Cintron back here." I looked at my classmates. Some of them were shaking their heads. Some were staring down at their desks.

"What's going on?" I asked.

"It was the test we took," said Ellenbeth.

"What about it?" I asked.

"Well, it made me think," said Ellenbeth.

"You're always thinking," I said.

"It made me think, too," said Louise Sinbad.

"And me."

"And me."

There was silence. I knew what my friends and classmates were talking about, but I didn't want to deal with it.

"Face it, Anya. Everybody misses Miss Cintron, but nobody really wants to force her to ruin her life by coming back here," said Helene.

"It wouldn't ruin her life," I insisted. "She likes us."

"It would ruin her dream," Helene said.

"It would ruin her special year."

"That's what I said on the test."

"Me, too."

"How did you answer the question, Anya?" Alice asked.

"How do you think? I'm not a selfish monster. I want Miss Cintron to be happy even if this turns out to be the worst year of my life."

"I wonder if we all gave the same answers on the other questions, too," Kathy said.

"No way. I bet Arthur said he wanted to travel to Disneyland," Helene teased. "I want to go to Iceland to study Icelandic comedy."

"For your information, I said Disney World," said Arthur.

Ellenbeth went to the wall of maps. "Disney World in Florida or France?" she asked.

"They have one in France?" Arthur sounded surprised.

Ellenbeth wrote Arthur's name on a slip of paper. "Go to France, Arthur," she said, and pinned it on the map near Paris. "This is Iceland." Ellenbeth stuck Helene's name in the center of a large island.

"I think you just stranded me on top of a glacier," said Helene.

"Hey, I said Disney World, too, but I wasn't really thinking," said Susan. "Put me in Egypt—near a pyramid."

Before long, the whole class was crowding around the maps, and soon there were colored pushpins and pieces of paper all over the world.

Shaundra Williams was the last kid to speak. "I don't want to go anywhere in the world."

"I can't believe you want to stay in Washingtonville your entire life," Ellenbeth said.

"Don't be ridiculous," said Shaundra. "I said the world, Earth. I want to be an astronaut. I want to explore space." Shaundra took her name tag and pinned it in the middle of the star map.

"I want to be a photographer," said Bettina, and started

chattering about how she wanted to spend her life crawling on her belly and hiding behind trees in the wilderness taking pictures of wild animals.

While she talked, I walked to the board. I was *not* going to be outdone by Ellenbeth. I started a list.

ASTRONAUT—1

PHOTOGRAPHER—1

It turned out that out of the twenty-five kids in 6-A, no two had the same goals. In our class were a future astronaut, and police officer, and scientist, and teacher, and detective, and veterinarian, and carpenter, and artist, and explorer, and plumber, and designer, and photographer, and nurse, and store owner, and general, and dancer—and the list went on and on.

"Impressive," said Ellenbeth, looking from the list to the maps and back again.

We all agreed. We were going to be an interesting bunch of people someday.

"What happened to Mr. Fred?" Alice asked.

"Yeah, where'd he go, Anya?" asked Aaron.

"Presidents don't know everything," I answered, looking under the teacher's desk.

"Who said anything about presidents? You were at the front of the room. Didn't you see him leave?"

"I was busy writing. Don't any of you have eyes?"

"Sometimes I wonder why I voted for you," Aaron complained.

"Too late now," said Helene.

"He's sleeping," said Mike from the back of the room.

"Where?" I asked.

"There," said Mike, pointing to the floor next to him.

"He's lying on the floor?" Alice looked interested. "Maybe he's dead."

Mike bent over to get a closer look. "No, he's breathing."

"Are we stuck with him for the rest of the year?" Kathy asked.

"No way."

"Who knows."

"Maybe."

"Probably."

"Probably?"

"It's Anya's fault."

"Wait a minute!" I interrupted my classmates. "You're going to blame me for Goldberg Fred?"

"Sure. If we hadn't been following your plan—" Kathy began.

"*My* plan? It was a class plan," I insisted.

"*Your* plan. You're responsible. You're president."

"That's it. I resign. You are now leaderless."

"I NOMINATE ANYA FOR CLASS PRESIDENT!" Helene shouted.

"I second it—I mean her," said Arthur.

"All in favor . . . ," said Helene.

The entire class said, "Aye."

"You're president again," said Helene.

"That took exactly one minute, seventeen seconds," said Alice, making a note in the log.

"What is this about?" I was never so frustrated in my life.

"We like having someone to blame," Helene explained.

Before I could say anything, the lunch bell rang.

Goldberg Fred leaped up from the floor, grabbed his tape player, put on a set of earphones, turned the volume way up, and marched out the door. We followed because we were hungry.

"I had fun this morning," said Arthur.

"Sure you did, *you* didn't get a C," Kathy whined.

"I had fun, too—after Mr. Fred fell asleep," said Louise.

"But the important thing is . . . ," said Alice, pausing until she had all of our attention.

"What?" we demanded.

"*He* didn't run the class—*we* did."

"Right. Snakeman took a nap," Kathy said. "We should report him."

"To who?" I asked.

"To *whom*," Ellenbeth corrected.

"I *hate* when you do that, Ellenbeth," I complained.

"We proved something important this morning," said Helene.

"What?" a few people asked.

"We don't need Mr. Fred."

"I thought you were starting to like him," I said.

"I think he's amusing, but we don't need him."

"Or any teacher," said Mike.

"We had a perfectly good geography lesson without the help of an adult," said Ellenbeth.

"That was geography? I liked it. We can teach ourselves from now on," said Arthur.

"I think that's illegal, Arthur," I said.

"I'm getting this all down in the log," said Alice. "It's evidence."

"It's unreadable," I said, looking over her shoulder as we tramped down the stairs.

"Tomorrow I'm bringing a camera," said Alice, ignoring me and continuing to write while walking.

"What's the point?"

"Evidence for Mr. Fred's court-martial," said Alice.

"You can only court-martial military people," said our future general.

"What can you do to bad teachers?"

"Drive them out of their minds."

"Goldberg Fred is already out of his mind."

"That's what we're going to prove. That's why I'm collecting evidence. When they read this and see a photo of Snakeface sleeping on the floor, and doing other strange things, they'll fire him." Alice waved the class log in the air.

"Maybe he'll be replaced by someone worse," said Helene.

"What's with you?" I asked.

"It's smart to cover all the possibilities," said Helene. "A snake in hand is safer than two in the bush."

"Ha, ha," I said. "Very funny. Besides, you just said we didn't need Goldberg Fred."

"She's conflicted," said Ellenbeth.

"What does that mean?" I asked.

"There is a conflict—an argument—a fight—going on inside Helene's head. She can't make up her mind about Mr. Fred," said Ellenbeth.

"I don't see why," I said.

By the time we reached the cafeteria, everyone was deep in thought.

"Another educational miracle—an orderly class 6-A. Nice work, Mr. Goldberg." Old Bad Breath was in his usual place at the cafeteria door.

"F-R-E-D, Fred, Mister Fred, Mister Goldberg *Fred*," corrected Goldberg Fred, who, without skipping a beat, guided us to the lunch line.

"How did he hear Pomeroy with music blasting in his ears?" asked Kathy.

"Good question. Maybe he never had music playing. Maybe he was pretending—so he could eavesdrop," I suggested.

"You mean he was listening to us the whole way to the cafeteria?" Alice hugged the log to her chest.

"Probably."

"Does that mean I'm in danger for plotting his end as our teacher?"

"The worst he can do is flunk you," said Kathy, "or maybe expel you—or leave you back."

Alice pulled a straw from her back pocket and landed a horrible, gooey spitball in the middle of Kathy's forehead.

"I'd call that argument a draw," said Goldberg Fred.

"Do you listen to everything?" Kathy complained.

Goldberg Fred smiled and wiggled his ears.

Spy from Space

9

After lunch we had physical education which, because of the weather, was held inside. By the end of the period, most of us were pretty cranky. We always are after indoor gym. When the bell rang, Mr. Fred showed up to take us to our classroom.

"I wonder what he did during his free period?" asked Bettina.

"Ate lunch probably," said Arthur.

"He ate with us. It's not normal," said Alice.

"No other teacher has actually eaten with us since Miss Cintron," said Mike.

"At least not voluntarily," said Ellenbeth.

"*Not at all*. Not a bite. Not a swallow," Mike insisted.

"Maybe Mr. Fred thought it was part of his job and was eating because he felt it was his duty to set a good example," suggested Lucile Evans, who always sees the best in people she doesn't know.

"I told him it wasn't," I said.

"Probably he just didn't believe you," said Lucile. "After all, you have been a ringleader in the effort to get rid of him." Lucy's kind of a split personality. She always sees the worst in people she knows.

"Stuff it, Lucy. I'm the class president, a leader, not a ringleader."

Helene interrupted. "Face it, everything Fred does is not normal."

"But he's funny, right? A real bucket of laughs," I said.

"Barrel, not bucket," Helene corrected. "I can't help if I'm conflicted, right Ellenbeth?"

"You're wishy-washy," I complained.

Helene said something that sounded like "harumph."

When we got back to our room, the shades were down, two screens had been hung behind Goldberg Fred's desk, and two projectors sat side by side on a table at the back of the room.

"Are we seeing slides or a movie?"

"It looks like both, cotton brain."

"Don't call *me* names, twit face."

"Shut up everyone, I have a headache," I complained.

"We all have headaches."

"It's the curse of gym in the gym," said Helene, cushioning her head in her hands.

"How can you make jokes?"

"That wasn't a joke."

"Why do they have to put three classes together?"

"Why did they build the gym out of cinder blocks? The sound bounces from wall to wall until it builds up speed, and then it goes into your ears and right to your brain, where it kills millions of important cells." Paul Saladino had just told us that morning he someday wanted to be a research biologist—or maybe a brain surgeon. "My career is finished," he lamented, rubbing his forehead with his fingers.

"You may stop the dramatics. No brain cells were destroyed during your physical education class unless one or more of you were whacked hard on the head. Anyone clobber you with a solid object, Mr. Saladino?"

Paul shook his head—gently.

"Did you run into any walls?"

"No," Paul mumbled.

"Then your career as a scientist is assured—providing you can get through sixth grade." Goldberg Fred ambled to the back of the room. Paul's face went blank—a sign that he was thinking dangerous thoughts.

"Lights!" directed Goldberg Fred. Someone flipped the light switch. "Camera! Action!" The slide and film show began. . . . Then it was over. The screen went dark.

The lights went on. I yawned. I looked around. Everyone was yawning. I looked at the clock. It was 2:55.

"We've been sitting here for more than an hour." My voice croaked as if I hadn't used it in years.

"An hour and twenty-five minutes to be exact," said Alice, trying to focus her eyes on the class log.

"It seemed like five minutes," said Mike.

"I saw this program about hypnotism—" began Ellenbeth.

"You weren't hypnotized, Miss Maggin, you were engrossed—interested—one might even say fascinated—the whole lot of you. Most likely, in time, you learning dodgers will remember that which you just witnessed as a turning point in your lives." Goldberg Fred's voice was mild and pleasant.

"Learning dodgers?" said Mike.

"Learning dodgers, education resisters, pedagogical malingerers—it all amounts to the same thing—"

Goldberg Fred was interrupted by the bell. There was a disorderly crush around our raincoats and boots. I was leaning against the closed door to our back room—the one with the sinks and tables and art supplies—trying to pull my rain boot over my sneaker, when I decided to try the knob. It wouldn't turn.

"I wonder why he's locked this door?" I mumbled.

"It's never even been closed before," Paul shielded his

mouth with the back of his left hand and spoke out of the side of his mouth.

"It has too," I said. "But it's never been locked."

"Do you have a toothache, Paul?" Helene asked.

Keeping his hand near his mouth, Paul spoke in a raspy whisper. "This isn't a laughing matter, Helene. I'm going undercover. You two meet me in the playground near the big tree." Paul turned up the collar of his raincoat and pulled his hat down over his eyes.

"It's pouring out there, Saladino. I'm not going to catch pneumonia because you've hatched another dumb idea." Helene started to leave.

"Then I'll do it without backup. Who needs chicken-livered partners anyway?" Paul slunk out of the coat-room.

"Do what? Partners for what?" I called after him. He ignored me.

"Oh boy," said Helene, "he's going to get into some kind of bad trouble."

"Slimy Fred got him really mad today. I think I'll catch up to Paul," I said.

"I guess I will, too," said Helene, tying a clear plastic rain bonnet over her yellow slicker hat.

"Do you have to wear two rain hats?" I asked.

"Yes. You know my mother insists."

"You look ridiculous," I said.

"Her theory is that I'll be dry even if one hat springs a leak."

"How come you changed your mind about going with Paul?" I asked.

"The same reason you're going with him. We've known him since kindergarten. We feel responsible."

"Can't you put one of those hats in your pocket and keep it as a spare?"

"No."

We met Paul under the big maple tree. "See, it's not that wet under here," he said. "Now, I'll follow him and you follow me—just in case."

"Who? Just in case of what?" I asked.

"Do I have to draw you a picture?" Paul complained out of the side of his mouth.

"No, just explain in words. And stop squinching your mouth over to the left side of your face," I said.

Paul twisted his mouth to the right side of his face and, using the back of his right hand to shield it, talked very fast.

"Did you understand a word he said?" I asked Helene.

"I think he said he's going to follow Goldberg Fred to his den of thieves—and then he said next of spies—no, I think it was nest of spies—and catch him in the woods—or maybe he said catch him with the goods. We're supposed to follow Paul and make sure Goldberg Fred doesn't—I think he said—'rub him out.'"

"Been watching too many of those old movies on TV, haven't you, Paul," I said. "Look, Goldberg Fred is a slimy rotten person, but he isn't a spy or a criminal."

"*You* said he's a spy, Anya. You *said* it to the whole class," Paul insisted.

"I meant a spy for Old Bad Breath—even a spy for other teachers—not a *real* spy—not a spy for another country. Besides, I thought you wanted to be a research biologist, not a detective," I said.

"Everyone needs a hobby," said Paul.

"I'm getting a chill, Anya. Let's go home," said Helene.

"Here he comes. If you don't want to help, don't," said Paul, flattening himself against the tree.

Goldberg Fred came down the main steps of the school and turned toward Albany Boulevard, our main street.

"What happens when he gets into his car, Paul?" I asked.

"Paul silently leaps onto the roof of the car and hitches a ride," said Helene.

"You think this is funny," Paul complained.

"No," said Helene, trying not to laugh.

Paul put his hands into his raincoat pockets and sauntered down the street after Goldberg Fred. We sloshed after Paul.

"What if Snake-faced Fred sees us?" asked Helene.

"It's a free country. We can walk where we want.

Besides, we're not following him, we're following the Great Saladino, master detective."

Goldberg Fred didn't get into a car. He walked down Albany Boulevard, stopping at the SuperRite Market, the hardware store, and Sam's Swell Shoes. He took his time at each place, coming out of the last wearing a pair of black rubber boots and carrying a large black umbrella in one hand and two clear-plastic shopping bags in the other.

"Oh swell, now his feet and his groceries are dry. He can wander around all afternoon." I was beginning to feel like a deep-sea diver—water wasn't exactly getting through my rain clothes, but my whole body felt cold and damp. I wanted to go home.

"Nothing is going to happen to Paul. Let's go home," I said.

"And give up right near the end?" said Helene.

"End of what?"

"My health, I think." Helene sneezed.

"Where'd they go?" I asked. Paul and Goldberg Fred had disappeared.

"Into another store?"

"Paul has been waiting outside stores."

We ran to the corner and looked both ways. There was no sign of either person.

"Uh-oh, we lost them," said Helene.

"More important, we lost Paul. Maybe Goldberg Fred snatched him after all."

"No, there's Paul, coming out of that alley. What's wrong with him?"

Paul looked totally out of it. His teeth were chattering and he could hardly speak. He pointed to the alley. It was a narrow space, about the width of a driveway. It was a dead end. There was nothing in the alley but a large puddle. In the middle of the puddle was a pile of rags.

"Goldberg Fred turned into a pile of rags?" I said, searching with my eyes for a possible escape.

"Are you sure he went into this alley?" asked Helene.

Paul nodded his head. The pile of rags moved slightly.

"The rags just moved," I said.

"Probably the wind."

"There *is* no wind. Look, it moved again."

"Those aren't rags. That's an animal. Don't go near it. It could be vicious or have rabies." Paul held onto our arms.

"Let go of me, Saladino. I want to see what it is."

"If it's wildlife, leave it alone. We'll call the humane society," said Paul.

"It's a dog, I think. It looks half dead. Maybe it's been hurt."

The soggy beast lifted its head and looked at me. Without thinking, I ran over to it, scooped it into my arms, and held it like a baby—which it seemed to be. It was a puppy—a long-haired, flop-eared, big-footed, wet, miserable puppy.

"I'm going home," I said.

"Your mother will never let you keep it," said Helene.

"Take it straight to the shelter," said Paul. "It could be diseased."

"Go back to being a detective, Saladino," I said, rushing along Albany.

"That's only my hobby. Science is my life. I know about stuff like microbes and germs and contagious things."

"Then go sterilize yourself. I'm taking this puppy home. Are you coming, Helene?"

"I wouldn't miss this for anything."

We got to my house. Paul was still with us. By this time we were all shivering. We went in through the garage, hanging our dripping coats on hooks and leaving our boots to make puddles on the floor. I put the puppy on the cement floor, but it wouldn't move. It just looked up at me and whimpered. I ran to get an armload of towels, and after rubbing most of the water out of its coat, I wrapped the dog in two of the softest towels and carried it into the kitchen.

"Hot chocolate," I said, putting the teakettle on the stove. We were all shivering.

"How about him?" asked Helene, pointing to the damp lump in my arms.

"We don't have any dog food, but we have lots of cat food," I said.

"Cat food does not have the right nutrition for dogs," said Paul.

"Then why don't you go out and buy dog food," I said.

"I will." And before we could stop him, Paul had gone into the garage, grabbed his coat, and headed for the small grocery store on the corner. He returned in minutes with two cans of dog food. "My treat," he said.

"That's very nice of you, Paul," Helene sounded surprised. One of Paul's nicknames is Mr. Cheap.

"I feel sorry for her."

"Who, the dog?" I asked.

"No, you. Wait until your mother gets her first veterinarian bill." Paul washed his hands carefully before drinking his hot chocolate.

The puppy wouldn't get up to eat, so I sat beside it and fed it tiny bits of the dog food. Walter, our extremely large orange cat, came into the kitchen, sniffed the puppy, and lay down next to it.

"I thought Walter hated all other animals," said Helene.

"I thought so, too," I said, petting a loudly purring Walter.

"It's probably a sign the dog is going to die," said Paul.

"You're a creep, Paul," said Helene.

"I just like to be scientific about things," he said.

"Then be scientific about Snake-faced Fred. Where did he go this afternoon?"

"I think he technically disappeared into thin air," said Paul.

"What do you mean by 'technically disappeared'?" I asked.

"It looked like he disappeared, but actually he didn't. He was either transported somewhere—"

"You mean like beamed up to a spaceship?" Helene asked.

"Yes, I do. Or he stepped through a portal in time."

"A portal?"

"A door into time . . ."

"Welcome to the Twilight Zone," said Helene.

". . . Or a portal to another dimension," Paul continued.

"Do-do-de-de-do-do-de-de . . . ," Helene sang.

"If you think you know so much, Holman, you tell us what happened to Goldberg Fred today," Paul demanded.

"Did you actually see him go poof?" Helene asked.

"Go poof?"

"You know, see him disappear. One second he's there and the next he's not."

"No."

"Then what happened is you lost him. That's all. You're a great scientist but a lousy detective," Helene said cheerfully.

"What about you, Anya? You were supposed to be my backup. Didn't you see where he went?"

"I guess we're all lousy detectives. Besides, what does it matter? You know I don't like him—and I don't trust him. He's a snakelike, slimy person—but that's all he is. The man is a teacher, not a spy from space." I winked at Helene and we both began laughing.

"Really?" said Paul. "Then tell me, what exactly did we do this afternoon in school, after gym?"

"We saw a movie and some slides and . . . and . . ." Helene stopped laughing.

"Can't really remember, can you?" said Paul.

"Yes I can," I said. "There were stars—it was a lesson about the universe—I think." Remembering was like trying to get a broken pair of binoculars to focus. Just as the image would start to get sharp, a tiny turn of the lens would make everything go fuzzy.

"Right, the universe. Space. Get it? *Space!*" Paul was right in my face.

The puppy was suddenly wide awake. It pushed itself between Paul and me and licked my face. I hugged it, and we rolled around on the floor for a while, wrestling.

"You sure know how to change a topic," Helene joked, grabbing the puppy around the neck and hugging it.

"You're both going to wind up getting rabies," Paul announced, moving out of our way as fast as possible.

10

ESP from Space

When we stopped playing, we realized that the puppy was starting to look pretty good. Dry, his fur was silky and soft. I got the old, half-full bottle of my father's after-shave lotion I had been hiding in the back of my closet. I rubbed it into the puppy's fur.

"You used too much," Helene complained, holding her nose.

"It'll fade when it dries," I said.

"I don't think so," said Paul. "Your father can probably smell it in Chicago."

"Don't talk about my father."

"I didn't say anything," said Paul.

"What are you going to call him?" asked Helene.

"Who, my father?"

"The dog, mushbrain. He needs a name."

"Duck."

"Duck?"

"Duck is his name."

"Well, you did find him in a puddle," said Paul.

"And he does have enormous feet," Helene added. "Good choice. I like it."

Actually, I had no idea why I said "Duck." It popped in my head, and once there, it seemed to fit the puppy perfectly.

Both Paul and Helene decided to stay around until my mother got home.

"You don't have to wait," I said.

"We *want* to wait. She's going to have a fit," said Helene. "I want to see it."

"You're wrong. My mother loves dogs."

"At other people's houses. She hates mess."

"She doesn't hate mess; she hates wasting time. Cleaning up messes wastes time. Besides, there is no mess. The towels are in the washing machine."

"What about housebreaking?" asked Paul.

"What about it?"

"Duck is going to make mistakes on the floor."

I hadn't thought about that. As if he understood us, Duck got up, went to the back door, and whined. I opened it and let him out.

"A genius dog," I said proudly.

"He's gone for sure. You should never let a dog out into an unfenced area without a leash—especially an untrained puppy—especially one who just moved in." As Paul spoke, Duck piddled in the yard and ran back to me. He bounded into the house wagging his very long tail.

"He's a perfect dog," I said.

"You'd better wipe his giant feet before your mother gets here," said Helene.

"Wipe whose giant feet?" My mother called from the hallway. "And has your father been here?"

"No, WHY?" I shouted back.

"Because this entire house stinks of that after-shave lotion he uses. I hate that smell." My mother walked into the kitchen. "You don't have to explain whose feet you were wiping. Is that your dog, Helene?" My mother bent down and scratched Duck behind the ears. He licked her.

"No, Mrs. Murray," said Helene.

"So it's your dog, Paul."

"No, Mrs. Murray."

"Uh-oh," said my mother.

"Isn't he cute?" I said. Duck tilted his head to the side and looked cute.

"He's going to be enormous. Look at those feet. Where did you get him?" My mother seemed to be taking Duck's presence very calmly.

"In an alley off Albany Boulevard."

"What were you doing in an alley off Albany Boulevard?" Now my mother sounded as if she could be starting to get angry.

"I have to go home now," said Paul, heading for the garage.

"Stop! Are you part of the explanation, Paul?" My mother gave Paul her famous squinty-eyed look of truth.

"I guess so," he mumbled.

"And how about you, Helene?"

"Sort of," said Helene.

My mother looked at her watch. "It's five-thirty. Do your parents know where you are?"

Sudden panic took over. "Stop running in circles. I'll call your parents."

My mother went into her bedroom to telephone the Saladinos and Holmans. When she came out she announced, "As punishment for not calling home, both of you are going to eat here tonight. You, Helene, are missing a lovely roast beef dinner, and you, Paul, are missing grilled pork chops and homemade ravioli—two of your favorite foods, I hear."

My mother went to the oven and turned it on. "Show them to the freezer, Anya," she ordered.

"Please, Mom, can't we make spaghetti or hamburgers or something else real?"

"Punishment is punishment," she said, smiling. "I

swore a mother's oath to their families. Grab me a turkey dinner and pick your own poison."

"What did your mother mean by that?" Paul asked, following me to the garage, the home of our giant freezer.

"It means we eat TV dinners tonight. Mrs. Murray hates them, but they save time," Helene whispered.

"I *love* TV dinners," said Paul. "We never get them at home."

"Shhhh," whispered Helene. "If Mrs. Murray finds out that we like them, she'll make us eat her cooking."

"What's wrong with my mother's cooking? The last time you ate here you stuffed your face pretty good."

"Be real, Anya. Spaghetti is the only food your mother cooks like a regular person. How about her Hamburgers Hawaiian or the soggy stuff she calls Tuna Wellington?"

"My mother is a frugal gourmet chef. You're just not used to fancy cuisine." I hate defending my mother's cooking. It really is awful.

"Frugal must mean you can't eat it," said Helene.

"Sometimes you are very unfunny, turtle breath. Frugal means it doesn't cost much. Now pick something to eat before everything defrosts." I opened the freezer door.

"Can I have fish sticks?" asked Paul, staring wide-eyed at the neat stacks of frozen foods.

"Are you sure?" I asked. Fish sticks are my least favorite—after Salisbury steak.

"I *never* get to eat fish sticks," said Paul, reaching for his choice.

"I think I'll have the Mexican combination," said Helene. I chose fried chicken for myself and took a turkey dinner for my mother.

When we got back to the kitchen, my mother was sitting on the floor with Duck curled in her lap. I poked Helene with my elbow and whispered, "I told you so."

"Sit," said my mother after we unboxed the dinners and put them in the oven. We sat. Knees touching, backs against the cabinets, we completely filled the little kitchen. "Explain."

We told her about our strange day with Goldberg Fred and how nasty and mean he had been. Paul tried to explain why it was important to follow Goldberg Fred. His reasons made about as much sense as they had the first time we heard them. Helene told my mother we followed Paul to keep him out of trouble, and I described Duck lying in the puddle.

"What happened to Mr. Fred?" my mother asked.

"He disappeared," said Paul.

"Well, he seems to have disappeared. Probably he just went inside a store or a building," I said.

"I saw him go into the alley. He didn't come out. There are no doors or windows at street level in that alley. He disappeared. Walked right through a portal . . ." Paul was pretty excited and deadly serious.

"A portal, Paul?" My mother buried her face between Duck's ears to keep Paul from seeing her smile.

"Yes. A time warp or an entrance into another dimension or something. Maybe it wasn't a portal. Maybe he was transported. . . ."

"He means beamed up, Mrs. Murray—like to the *Enterprise*," said Helene.

"I understand what he means. This Mr. Fred sounds like an unusual man, but to tell you the truth, Paul, it is doubtful that he is from another planet—or another time—or another dimension. The odds against any of those three possibilities must be a zillion to one. Maybe we can come up with other answers during dinner." My mother stood up, brushed the dog hair off her slacks, and excused herself.

"Your mother didn't throw a fit." Helene was disappointed.

"I told you so," I said, but I was surprised myself.

"What other answers could there be?" Paul asked.

"What are you talking about?" asked Helene.

"Mr. Fred."

"Oh him."

"He's just completely sneaky, Paul. Somehow he got out of sight without you seeing him." I really wanted to believe what I was saying.

Paul looked as if he were going to burst, and then he blurted out, "I think Goldberg Fred can read minds."

"Yeah, well . . ." I couldn't believe Paul had said that.

"Yeah, well? That's all you have to say, Anya? Paul is going right off the deep end—bonkers forever and ever —and all you have to say is 'yeah, well.' Listen Paul, mind reading is a trick stage magicians do. People can't read minds." Helene stood up, grabbed the receiver from the kitchen wall phone, and dialed.

"Hello, Ellenbeth? People can't actually read minds, can they? No, I'm not eating Silly Putty; this is a serious question. I'll explain tomorrow." Helene was quiet for about five minutes while Ellenbeth talked. When she hung up, she didn't look very confident. "Ellenbeth said it's possible."

"That Mr. Fred can read minds?" said Paul.

"That a person can have something called ESP . . ."

"Extrasensory perception," said Paul gleefully. "The ability to read thoughts or sense feelings or move objects with your mind or—"

"If you knew all this, why didn't you tell us?" Helene was bugged.

"I *tried* to tell you, but you had to call Ellenbeth to see if she saw it on television."

"Well, where did *you* learn about this ESP stuff?" Helene demanded.

"From books."

"It's in books?" Helene was surprised.

"Of course it's in books. Most things are," said Paul.

"So Goldberg Fred is just an ordinary person who maybe has some ESP." I was relieved.

"You don't sound surprised, Anya," Helene said.

"I'm not."

"Has he been in your mind, too?" asked Paul.

"Most definitely. I thought I was imagining it—or going crazy."

"You're both crazy."

"Why are they both crazy?" My mother was back. "Did you set the table?"

As we put out tableware and napkins, we told my mother about the ESP and Goldberg Fred.

"Just because a human might have ESP doesn't mean that Mr. Fred is human—or even from our time or space," Paul insisted. "ESP is one thing, but disappearing is another."

"Did anyone think of cooking a dinner for Duck?" my mother asked.

"We fed him dog food," I said.

"But he'd love to eat something else," said my mother.

"How do you know?" I asked.

"I just do. Duck and I have a good rapport, don't we, boy?" Duck sat on my mother's foot and stared lovingly into her eyes. My mother went to the refrigerator, took out some chopped meat, and made two large hamburger patties. She heated a pan and began cooking them.

"Those can't be for Duck," I said.

"Why not?" asked Paul.

"Because of our budget. We were going to make meat loaf tomorrow. Those dog burgers are half of my week's beef ration," I complained.

"You exaggerate," said my mother, flipping the meat.

"Why are you cooking the meat if it's for Duck?" asked Helene.

"Raw meat is not particularly good for dogs and cats," said Paul.

"He likes it cooked," said my mother.

"How do you know?" I said.

"Take the dinners out of the oven, Anya. Use the mitts."

We sat down to eat—Duck on the kitchen floor with a dish of hamburgers and us around the table in the dining corner of the living room with TV dinners.

"This is delicious, Mrs. Murray," said Paul. Helene kicked him under the table.

"It is?" My mother looked at our dinners and shook her head. "I think I'll start making big pots of homemade stews and soups and freezing portions of them," she said. "It'll be more economical, more nutritious, and better tasting than this stuff."

"It'll take lots of time to cook all that stuff," I said.

"We'll spend one Saturday a month cooking for the entire month. It will save time in the end. Now what about this Mr. Fred problem. Have you—" The phone rang, interrupting my mother. She motioned for us to continue eating and went into the kitchen. When she came out, she was holding Duck in her arms. She looked upset.

"What's wrong, Mom?" I asked.

"He's coming for his dog." My mother looked teary-eyed.

"Who's coming for his dog?" I asked.

"Him. That Mr. Fred person. He says Duck is his dog and he's coming to take him home." Duck licked my mother's face as she put him on the floor.

"How did he know Duck was here?"

"How do we know Duck is really his dog?"

"He doesn't deserve to have a puppy like Duck."

"Finish your dinners, kids." My mother picked up her fork and moved the beige food from one side of her plate to the other.

"I'm not hungry anymore," I said.

"I'm finished," said Paul, eating the last pea on his plate. "Do you want the rest of yours, Helene?" he asked.

"Yes," she said, pulling her food away from him.

"You can have my chicken," I offered. In minutes, except for my mother's plate, there wasn't a leftover on the table.

"Clear away the dishes and I'll make some coffee."

"You're going to give coffee to a dog-snatching fiend?" I asked.

"Technically, if Duck is his, you snatched his dog. On the other hand, I am curious to know how the man knew we had the dog . . . *and* how he knew the dog's name." My mother walked into the kitchen. We crowded in after her.

"He knew Duck's name, Mom?"

"Are you sure you didn't mention it first, Mrs. Murray?" asked Helene.

"I am positive. I said, Hello. He asked, Is this the Murray residence? I said, Yes. He said, I am Mr. Goldberg Fred, your daughter's teacher, and I think you have my dog Duck at your house." My mother filled the coffee machine with water.

"This is spooky," said Helene.

"Weird," I added, nervously.

"ESP from outer space," said Paul, looking at Duck suspiciously.

Duck sat back on his hind quarters and waved his enormous, floppy front paws in the air. I could have sworn he winked at me.

Duck, the Frinch Puddle

11

When the doorbell rang, Duck leaped to his feet and raced in circles, barking.

"He's loud," said Helene, putting her hands over her ears. "He sounds gigantic."

"He sounds like he has the teeth of a piranha," Paul added.

"Duck would have been nice protection for us," my mother sighed.

"Aside from his looks, he does seem just about perfect," said Paul.

"He looks fine to me. Get out of my way." I pushed Paul.

"Hey," he complained as he stuck out his foot to trip me.

"That's enough, you two. Go wait in the living room. Take Duck with you. I'll get the door," my mother ordered.

"Come, Duck," I said. Duck ignored me. He was following my mother, growling. I jumped in front of him, blocking his way. "Come with me, Duck. I'll give you a treat." Duck tried to get around me. I picked him up and carried his struggling body into the living room, where I put him on the floor and lay down on top of him. "Stay," I commanded.

"Doesn't sound as if he likes Goldberg Fred very much," said Helene.

"Who does?" I asked. Duck snarled.

My mother and Goldberg Fred came through the doorway. "Good, Duck's still here," he said.

"How did you know I found Duck?" I asked.

"Through simple deductive reasoning. I saw you following me today."

"Please be seated, Mr. Fred," my mother's voice was polite and cold. "I'll get us some coffee."

"You don't have to bother, Mrs. Murray. I'll just take Duck home with me."

"No, Mr. Fred, you won't. We will have some coffee, or tea if you prefer, while we find out if this dog is actually yours. He doesn't seem to like you very much."

"Coffee will be fine," said Goldberg Fred, settling himself on the sofa. "But I don't see how Duck could be anyone's dog but mine. What makes you think he doesn't like me?"

Duck looked at Goldberg Fred and began growling, snarling, and whining.

"He hates you," I said, holding onto Duck so he wouldn't leap at Goldberg Fred's throat. "If he *is* your dog, you must have been terrible to him."

"You do have an excellent imagination, Miss Murray," said slimy Fred.

My mother came in carrying a tray. She didn't say a word as she set the tray on the low table and sat down at the opposite end of the sofa from Goldberg Fred. I reached for a cookie and Duck escaped. Screaming a horrible death cry, he leaped straight into the air and seemed to fly over the coffee table. He landed on Goldberg Fred's head.

"Dial 911," Helene yelled.

Goldberg Fred pushed Duck onto the sofa. Duck leaned his body against Goldberg Fred and continued to growl and whine. His lip curled back over his teeth. It was a truly ugly and frightening sight.

"You shouldn't get on furniture without asking permission," said Goldberg Fred.

Duck snarled. Goldberg Fred stuck his face right into

Duck's, so Duck's gleaming, white choppers were snapping about an inch from his nose.

"The man is nuts," said Paul.

"I told you to call 911," whispered Helene.

Goldberg Fred turned his head toward us. For a second he looked puzzled and then he smiled. "Of course. You think Duck is exhibiting hostility toward me because of the noise he's making—and his display of teeth. It's just that you're not used to him or members of his species. All Frinch Puddles sound this way when they use their voices to communicate."

"French Poodle? Who's he kidding?" said Helene.

"His species? Duck is a dog, a canine, isn't he?" asked Paul.

"Of course he is, Mr. Saladino. I misspoke myself. I meant breed. Duck is a member of a rare and unusual breed." Goldberg Fred patted the lip-curling Duck on the head. Duck threw his head back and howled.

"What did you mean by 'use their voices' to communicate? As opposed to what—mental telepathy?" I realized what I had said and clamped my hand over my mouth. I didn't want Goldberg Fred to know we suspected him—or anyone, even a dog—of having ESP.

Goldberg Fred ignored my comment. "Duck is a *Frinch Puddle*, not a French Poodle."

"There's no such breed of dog," Paul insisted.

"Are you familiar with *all* breeds of dogs, Mr. Saladino? Can you identify an Anatolian Shepherd or a Tibetan Terrier? Have you ever heard of the Neapolitan Mastiff, the Canaan Dog, the Pharoah Hound, the Ibizan Hound—to name just a few of the more uncommon breeds? How can you say there is no such thing as a Frinch Puddle when a fine example of the breed sits in front of your very nose." Goldberg Fred scratched Duck under the chin.

"What exactly *is* a Frinch Puddle dog, Mr. Fred?" My mother's voice sounded as if it had acid dripping from it.

"He's ticking her off," Helene whispered.

"Why should she be different from everyone else?" I whispered back.

"Duck is a perfect example of a Frinch Puddle. Stand up, Duck, and show yourself off." Goldberg Fred moved over. Duck stood up and turned around slowly so we could view his floppy ears and pointy nose and huge feet and short legs and amazingly long, shaggy tail. Then, with a big sigh, he flopped onto his stomach and closed his eyes.

"This is ridiculous, Mr. Fred," said my mother.

"Don't you think Duck is a fine dog?" Goldberg Fred sounded hurt. Duck opened one eye and looked at my mother.

"I *love* Duck—we all do, but it's obvious he's simply a nice mutt."

"A mutt? Duck?" Goldberg Fred sounded shocked. Duck opened both eyes and growled.

"A mixed breed. A combination of a number of varied ancestors. I am not insulting Duck, I am describing him."

"No you're not, Mrs. Murray. Duck is pure Frinch Puddle. On his home . . . island, Frinch Puddles are known for their hunting abilities. They are the only creatures in the . . . world, who are able to lie in puddles for hours—or even days—in order to catch the fierce Puddle Shark." Goldberg Fred calmly stirred cream into his coffee.

Helene started giggling. Even Paul smiled a little.

"And where exactly is Frinch—or is it Franch?" my mother asked. The acid was gone from her voice.

"She's got him now," said Paul.

"No she hasn't," I said. I knew my mother. She was starting to enjoy herself.

"What do you mean?" Paul asked.

"She thinks he's kidding around. My mother likes humorous people," I whispered.

"So?" said Paul.

"So she's not on our side anymore."

"When did you start believing that humor is dangerous?" whispered Helene.

"I don't believe that," I whispered back.

"The man is funny, Anya. Face it. Funny isn't your enemy—Fred is."

"Frence is a long way from here," said Goldberg Fred.

"France? A Frinch Puddle from France?"

"Not France, Frence—F-R-E-N-C-E. France has poodles. Frence has puddles."

"I'm sure there must be at least a few puddles in France, Mr. Fred," my mother quipped.

"Puddles, yes. Frinch Puddles, no, Mrs. Murray."

"And just where exactly is this place Frence, home of the remarkable Frinch Puddle dog? In Europe? In Asia? In South America? In Africa? Hidden somewhere in North America? Perhaps tucked away in a corner of Australia? You did mention it was an island. An island in a sea, an ocean, a lake?" My mother grinned.

"Would you like to teach a geography lesson to my students?" said Goldberg Fred. "You really know your stuff."

"Thank you," my mother took a sip of coffee, "but you are not going to change the topic. Where is Frence on a map of the world?"

"Actually, Frence is out of this world . . . ," said Goldberg Fred.

"I TOLD YOU!" Paul shouted.

My mother gave Paul a bad look. Paul shut up. Goldberg Fred continued. "For the sake of this discussion, let's just say Frence is a state—of mind."

"Ah, a fine place for Duck to come from." My mother was now giving rotten Fred a toothy smile.

Goldberg Fred smiled back at my mother and finished his cup of coffee.

"On the phone, how did you know I named the dog Duck?" I demanded.

"I didn't know you named Duck Duck, but since that is his name, it makes sense," said Goldberg Fred.

"No it doesn't," I said. "Something smells around here."

Goldberg Fred leaned over and sniffed Duck's head. "You're right. Duck smells like rotting vegetation."

My mother laughed.

"That's not what I mean," I said, glaring at my mother.

"You're being rude, Anya," my mother snapped.

"I thought you were on my side," I said.

"Always," said my mother, but she didn't sound as if she meant it.

"I named my Frinch Puddle Duck for two reasons—the size and shape of his giant feet and his habit of lying in the middle of any puddle big enough to—well, any large puddle. In Frence, Duck is a common name for Frinch Puddles because they all share those characteristics.

"Why did *you* begin calling Duck, Duck?" Goldberg Fred asked.

"Because of his feet and the puddle, I guess," I mumbled.

"How come Duck was outside on such a terrible day?

Some people shouldn't be allowed to keep dogs," said Paul.

"I agree. Duck sneaked around me when I walked through my door. As soon as I realized he was missing, I went looking for him. After searching every wet spot in the entire downtown area, I thought that perhaps you might have seen him and rescued him. So I called, and here he is and here am I."

"As much as I would like to keep Duck, this all makes sense to me," said my mother.

"*No!*" I insisted.

Duck climbed off the sofa and came over to me. I hugged him and said, "If you knew we were following you, why didn't you say something to us?"

"Why? You weren't bothering me, and as far as I know, it's not against the law to skulk around in the rain. Thank you for the coffee, Mrs. Murray. Let's go, Duck."

"Skulk?" said Helene.

"Look it up," said Goldberg Fred.

"WHERE DO YOU LIVE?" shouted Paul. "I didn't see you go through any door. You walked into an alley and disappeared."

"If I disappeared, how could I be here now?" Goldberg Fred asked. My mother embarrassed me by laughing.

"You know what I mean," said Paul. "You disappeared through a portal."

"I did, indeed, walk through the portal leading to my home—although portal usually implies a somewhat larger entryway." Goldberg Fred wiggled a finger at Duck. Duck made some noises and ambled to the front door. "Duck says good night and thanks. He particularly enjoyed the dog food and hamburgers. He wants to know if he can visit here again."

"Anytime," said my mother, shutting the door behind the strange pair.

"Hey, how did he know what Duck ate here?" I said.

"It makes sense that we would feed a dog dog food," said my mother.

"How about the hamburgers?" I asked. "Nobody mentioned hamburgers."

"Probably someone did," said my mother. "Or maybe he just smelled them in the air."

"No way. Something is rotten here," I said.

"It's just the smell of the swamp-water after-shave lotion."

"Very funny, Helene." I was missing Duck and feeling sorry for myself. I've always wanted a dog of my own, and for a couple of hours, I thought I finally had one.

"I think you kids would get along much better with Mr. Fred if you took some time to understand his dry sense of humor. You're so angry with him for not being Miss Cintron that you won't give him a chance. Now help me with these dishes, and I'll drive Helene and Paul home." My mother looked sad as she picked up Duck's water bowl from the kitchen floor.

"What's a dry sense of humor?" asked Paul.

"One that isn't funny to most people," I said.

"It figures," said Paul.

Teacher from Somewhere

12

By Tuesday morning the rain had stopped. My mother, who didn't trust either the weather report or the actual sun shining in a cloudless sky, made me wear my rain boots to school. I felt like an idiot.

Helene caught up to me in front of My Dear Watson. "If you're afraid of falling into puddles, maybe you should wear a life preserver instead of rubber boots."

"She who wears two rain hats shouldn't talk fashion," I said.

"At least I wear them when it's raining." Helene jumped over a large puddle to avoid the punch I aimed at her arm. I was thrown off balance and stumbled into the middle of the muddy pool.

"See where your temper gets you?" said Helene. "Up to your neck in dirty water."

"It's only ankle-deep," I grumbled. As I slogged to the other side, water sloshed over the tops of my boots.

"Hah!" I said.

"Hah what?" Helene asked.

"Because of these stupid boots, I wound up in the middle of a pond. My socks are wet. I'm going to catch cold and get tropical foot rot and waste a whole lot of my mother's time."

"You got wet because of your rotten disposition, not your boots. I think this Goldberg Fred thing is starting to make your mind scramble," said Helene.

"My mind is as unscrambled as yours," I said as we reached the playground and our classmates.

"A self-admitted omelette brain." Helene giggled and backed away from me.

"Sometimes what you think is your sense of humor gets on my nerves," I complained.

Goldberg Fred told us to line up alphabetically, by first names. I was forced to stand next to Alice, who was carrying a bulky object wrapped in brown paper.

"Did you make another weapon, Alice?" I asked.

"A catapult," she answered proudly.

"A cat what?" asked Arthur.

"A catapult. Catapults were invented to be war machines. They were first used by the ancient Greeks and

Romans to throw stones, darts, and arrows at their enemies."

"I saw a cata-watcha-ma-call-it in a movie about olden times," said Arthur. "Guys in metal suits were trying to break into a castle using one of those things—but it was a whole lot bigger than what you've got there."

"Guys in metal suits? Sounds like a science fiction movie I saw—*Attack of the Mutant Robots*," said Aaron.

"Arthur's talking about medieval times and knights in armor," said Alice. "They came a long time after the ancient Greeks and Romans."

"And way before the mutant robots," said Helene.

Alice ignored her. "Catapults of different designs were popular for hundreds of years." Alice unwrapped her catapult.

"Isn't that a little small to break down castle walls?" I asked.

"Looks just like a slingshot to me," said Aaron.

"A slingshot is a miniature catapult," said Alice.

"The original slingshots—which didn't look anything like the one you have there—are older than catapults," said Ellenbeth from down the line. "People didn't have elastic back then. I saw this program—"

A couple of kids groaned, and Ellenbeth went into one of her snits of silence. It would be at least a day before she would give us any useful information.

"Alice must spend all her spare time building weapons—pretty twisted if you ask me," said Lucy.

Alice turned toward the prissy, critical voice and snapped the elastic on her miniature catapult. "Nobody asked you, Lucile." Then she removed a foam rubber ball from her pocket, squirted something onto it, and slipped it into the sling. Lucy ducked behind Louise just as Alice swiveled on her heel and took aim at the back of Goldberg Fred's head.

At that moment, Goldberg Fred turned around. "It looks as if Alice, our class assassin, has produced another instrument of destruction. How nice." Goldberg Fred lifted the little catapult from Alice's hand and without seeming to aim, shot the foam rubber ball across the playground. It landed in the middle of Mr. Pomeroy's back and stayed there, stuck to his suit jacket. The class made a whooshing noise as everyone sucked in air at the same moment. We froze in place waiting for Old Bad Breath to come get us, but he didn't seem to notice he'd been attacked. There was a loud sigh as we all began breathing again.

"Good choice of missile. Lightweight but capable of traveling through space in a direct line. What kind of glue did you use?" Goldberg Fred handed Alice the slingshot.

Alice put her hands behind her back, refusing to take it. "Crazy Glue. It'll never come off," she whispered.

"Some of it will, but he's going to have little bits of foam rubber stuck to his jacket forever," Lucy cackled.

"Shut up, Lucy," Helene warned.

"Don't you want your weapon, Alice? It's nicely constructed." Goldberg Fred held it in front of Alice's nose. She shook her head and backed away a step. Goldberg Fred slipped the slingshot into his pocket.

"How come nobody is saying anything to Old Bad Breath?" Aaron asked as Mr. Pomeroy walked between lines of students and teachers with the small, bright, orange ball gently bobbing up and down in the center of his back. "That's not exactly invisible."

"Don't point," Alice hissed.

"Maybe they think it's a fashion statement. The executive polka dot," said Helene. "Perfect for brightening up that drab, grey business suit."

"Witty, Miss Holman," said Goldberg Fred. He turned to Aaron. "Most of the time, people don't notice things. They tend to pass through the world without actually focusing on what is happening around them. Consequently, small details—and potentially large discoveries —are overlooked every day."

"Like the detail that it was you who messed up Pomeroy's suit, not Alice." Kathy spoke from down the line.

"Did I, Miss Pepper? Did you actually see me work the weapon, or are you simply guessing?"

"I saw you do it," I said. "Alice is innocent."

"What constitutes innocence, Miss Murray? Did Alice construct the weapon? Did she bring it to school with her? Did she provide ammunition? Did she coat the ammunition with glue? Did she load the weapon? How innocent is she? I simply took the weapon from her just as it accidentally fired and hit poor, unfortunate Mr. Pomeroy." Goldberg Fred smiled sadly.

"Slingshots don't fire by accident. Someone has to pull the elastic," said Arthur.

"But first there has to be elastic to pull," said Goldberg Fred.

The bell rang and we headed for the school.

"What would have happened if it had been a dangerous weapon, like a bow and arrow?" asked Bettina.

"Or a gun?" someone whispered.

That shut us all up until we got to our room.

"People hunt and kill animals with slingshots," said Ellenbeth, forgetting she was mad at us.

"So what?" said Bettina.

"So slingshots are dangerous. They're real weapons, like guns. That's so what."

"SHUT UP, EVERYONE! I'M NOT AN ASSASSIN!" Alice shouted.

"You are, too. You're always making weapons to hurt people," Lucy whined.

Alice pointed to the blowgun on the wall. "That's a hunting tool. It was invented to feed people, not hurt them. Besides, the only ammunition I ever shoot is harmless."

"Tell that to the person wiping your germ-filled spitballs off his face," said Paul.

"On the playground, you defined catapults as weapons of war," said Goldberg Fred.

"But what I made is really a slingshot, not a catapult, and slingshots have always been used for hunting, not war," Alice insisted.

"Perhaps in some parts of the world," said Goldberg Fred, removing Alice's slingshot from his pocket. "However, I haven't noticed any hunting expeditions at My Dear Watson. Perhaps you are intending to stalk the elusive wild hamburger or bring down the fleet-footed pizza slice in order to feed yourself and your classmates this lunch hour."

The class began to laugh. We watched as Goldberg Fred put an object into the sling, pulled back on it, aimed, and fired.

I hit the floor as something whizzed over my desk. There was a loud thunk. I sat up in time to see that half the class was on the floor. The laughter had stopped.

"ARE YOU NUTS?" Alice screamed. She was closest to the wall of maps, where there was now a fair-sized hole in the bulletin board—right in the middle of Antarctica. She stuck her ballpoint pen into the hole and dug around for a few seconds.

"A ROCK!" she shouted, holding a small rock for all of us to see. "The man is a menace. He shot a rock at me."

"A mere pebble, Miss Greenbaum," said Goldberg Fred. "And it was aimed exactly where it landed."

"Why are you calling me Miss Greenbaum?"

"I thought that was your name. Am I mistaken?"

"Drop it, Alice," I suggested. "The point is that *he* shot a weapon in a room full of kids—*us*."

"Something Miss Greenbaum has done hundreds of times," said Goldberg Fred, "with encouragement from all of you."

"Alice just uses the weapons to annoy teachers," said Mike.

"And us, when she's bored," said Louise.

"We don't encourage her to shoot us," said Arthur.

"Ah, so it's just fine and dandy to shoot a weapon in this room as long as you, personally, approve of the target." Goldberg Fred smiled his awful smile at us.

"Alice has never used deadly ammunition, like rocks," I said.

"Germs can be deadlier than any rock," said Goldberg Fred. "Perhaps Miss Greenbaum is more sophisticated in her assassination plans than you suspect."

"I AM NOT CONDUCTING GERM WARFARE! I AM NOT AN ASSASSIN!" Alice shouted again. She was close to tears.

I stood up. I hated when everyone ganged up on one

kid. "Stop picking on Alice," I demanded. "We have more important things to talk about."

"You're getting awfully good at giving orders," Lucy complained.

"Thank you," I said.

"That's not what—" Lucy began.

Paul interrupted Lucy. "What's more important, Anya?"

"Him," I said, pointing to Goldberg Fred.

"Thank you," said Goldberg Fred.

I ignored him and continued. "Do any of you remember yesterday afternoon, after gym?"

"We saw a movie," said Louise.

"A slide show," said Mike.

"Both," said Paul.

"And what exactly were they about?" I asked.

There was silence. Goldberg Fred leaned against the chalkboard and tried to look innocent.

"Aha!" I said. "We've lost a chunk of time, and none of us can remember what happened to us."

"What does it mean, Anya?" Susan sounded worried.

"Tell everyone how we know Goldberg Fred is from another planet, or another time, or dimension," Paul was on his feet.

"Do you know that, Anya?" Kathy asked. A couple of kids started sniggering.

"No, I don't know that. What I do know is that he"
—I pointed to Goldberg Fred—"can get into our heads
and read our thoughts and make us lose part of an
afternoon."

"Inside our heads?" said Crazy Arnold, sounding more
interested than worried.

"What do you think happened to us yesterday afternoon?" asked Bettina.

"Maybe we were beamed up to a spaceship and examined by space creatures," Shaundra suggested, giggling nervously.

"Inside *my* head and read *my* thoughts?" Crazy Arnold
was getting excited.

"This is stupid," said Ellenbeth. "According to doc-
umentaries I've seen, all reports about people from space
describe them in the same way. They have big heads and
huge eyes and are very short."

"Well, a couple of years ago some Russian kids saw
eleven-foot-high space people with almost no heads," said
Louise.

"There are no such things as space people," said Kathy.
"And if there were, they wouldn't be people. They'd
be . . ."

"What proof do you have to support that conclusion?"
All eyes turned to Goldberg Fred. A number of mouths
dropped open.

"Are you admitting that you're some kind of space creature?" I asked in amazement.

"I admit nothing."

"But is there anything to admit?" asked Aaron.

"He said he admits nothing," said Lucy.

"You can admit nothing while knowing a whole lot," said Aaron.

"WHAT DO YOU MEAN HE GETS INSIDE OUR HEADS!" Crazy Arnold shouted.

"He reads minds. He read Anya's mind and my mind and—" Helene began.

"He could simply be an earthling who is telepathic," said Ellenbeth.

"Earthling?" Mike began laughing. "Maybe he's a Martian—or the man in the moon. Beam me up, Ellenbeth."

"Mars is probably too cold to support life," someone mumbled.

"And Venus is too hot, and the air is mostly carbon dioxide," said Louise. "You couldn't breathe on Venus."

"So what?" said Mike.

"So Venus is the planet closest to us. Maybe Goldberg Fred comes from another galaxy."

"A galaxy has billions of stars in it. Maybe he comes from a planet in our galaxy, but not in our solar system," Paul added.

"That narrows it down to about 100 billion stars," I said. "Wait a second. How do I know that? How do any of you know any of what you just said?"

"What are you talking about, Anya?" asked Louise.

"How do I know that a light-year is how far light travels in a year at a rate of 186,281.7 miles a second?"

"That comes out to be five trillion, eight hundred and eighty billion miles," said Susan.

"How do you know that?" I demanded. "You're terrible at math."

"Stars are so far away that it's sometimes easier to explain the distance by using parsecs. A parsec is 3.26 light-years or 19.2 trillion miles," said Crazy Arnold. Then he got a really funny look on his face and began shouting. "ANYA'S RIGHT! I DON'T KNOW THIS STUFF, BUT IT'S INSIDE MY HEAD!" Then, instead of doing something really Arnold-like and bizarre, he said, "neat," and sat down smiling.

"What do you mean, neat? This is proof something strange and horrible is going on because of him!" I pointed to Goldberg Fred.

"No, Anya. We're just remembering the stuff that was in the film and slide show yesterday," said Lucy. "You're making trouble as usual."

"She is not." Paul defended me. "We may have learned this yesterday, but how come we didn't know we learned it until a few minutes ago?"

We all turned to look at Goldberg Fred. He looked back at us. Finally Mike broke the silence.

"We were hypnotized by him. It was extraterrestrial brainwashing." Mike hit his desk to make his point.

"But we learned good stuff," said Arthur, "like our eyes can't register the wavelengths of all the things that are going on in space. Mostly we can see the white light of the stars. But special cameras can pick up colors and movement and explosions. What we saw in the movie looked like the best fireworks show in the world. The universe is . . . is . . . fantastic."

"It must be brainwashing if all that came out of Arthur's mouth," Helene mumbled.

"And the universe is so huge and stars are so far apart that it's impossible for Goldberg Fred to come from anywhere but Earth," said Ellenbeth.

"Wrong," I said. "The universe is filled with thousands of billions of stars. How many of those stars have planets around them? What makes you think that Earth is the only place with intelligent life?"

"What about God?" someone whispered.

"I believe that God is everywhere, including out there," Paul pointed to the star map on the wall.

"Stick to the subject. There's something strange going on in this classroom," I said.

"What if someone doesn't believe in God?" Louise asked.

"What does that have to do with what we're talking about?" I was getting very annoyed.

"Nothing really. I just asked."

"You know, what I saw yesterday made me feel tiny, like a speck of dust." Lucy was almost whispering.

"It made me feel enormous and important and part of something amazing," said Helene, serious for once.

"This conversation is getting us nowhere. I think I'd better tell you what happened to me and Anya and Helene yesterday," said Paul.

"Not a good idea, Paul," I warned. "They're going to think we're nuts."

"No, they're not." Paul told the class about how we followed Goldberg Fred. When he got to the part where he insisted that Goldberg Fred disappeared through a portal, I put my head down on my desk.

Helene poked me. "Why are you hiding, Anya? You already told the class that you thought Goldberg Fred has been controlling our minds. Portals aren't a whole lot stranger than that, are they?"

"I guess not." I picked up my head to look at my classmates. No one was laughing at Paul.

"Maybe he was beamed up to a spaceship," suggested Arthur.

"Another possibility," said Paul.

A few impolite snorts could be heard.

"Don't mix science fiction with fact," said Bettina.

"Goldberg Fred is from outer space," Paul insisted.

"Prove it," said Goldberg Fred.

"What did he say?" asked Aaron.

"He said prove it."

"What?"

"Are you serious?"

"Prove what?"

"That he's an alien."

"Or a time traveler."

"Who said anything about time travel?"

"I just did."

"Exactly what do you mean?" I asked Goldberg Fred.

"Exactly what I said. Prove that we are not exactly from around here."

"We? There are more than one of him?" A nervous voice squeaked from the back of the room.

"We—Duck, my dog, and me. He's part of your theory too, isn't he, Mr. Saladino?"

"Yes," said Paul.

Goldberg Fred whistled and Duck came bounding in from the back room.

"Duck's been here all morning?" I said.

"Yes, he's learned to open the portal—as Mr. Saladino calls my door—by himself. It's too dangerous leaving him home alone, so he's going to spend the rest of the term with us as part of this project."

"Dogs aren't allowed in the school," Lucy whined.

"Don't be a pain, Lucile," I said. Duck had come over and was leaning his chin on my knee.

"Anyone tells on this dog, and they have to deal with me," said Arthur.

"And me," I added.

"And me," said Helene and Paul.

"And by all means don't forget me, your teacher from space—or somewhere," said Goldberg Fred.

Duck leaped into Goldberg Fred's arms and smiled at the class. It was a horrible sight to see.

The Project

Is that dog dangerous?" Lucy couldn't take her eyes off Duck's teeth.

Duck wiggled out of Goldberg Fred's arms, scrambled onto Lucy's desk, lay down, rolled over, and waved his huge paws in the air.

"Does he look dangerous?" asked Helene.

Lucy could barely shake her head. She seemed frozen with fear. Duck licked her face, then turned to Helene and winked. Helene winked back.

"That dog winked at Helene." Bettina sounded worried.

"That is not exactly a dog," I said.

"Look, doesn't it bother any of you that for weeks and

weeks we've been coming to a fun house instead of a school? We don't learn anymore. I mean next year we're going to be in junior high, and we won't be prepared. Goldberg Fred is a teacher. That is a dog. And we all know that Miss Cintron isn't coming back. Maybe we should just get to work—be students again." Ellenbeth was wringing her hands with nervousness.

"What's wrong with you, Ellenbeth? We have an alien, no, two aliens in our classroom, and you're worried that we're not learning stuff?" Mike asked.

"I think Ellenbeth is suffering from educational underload," said Helene.

"Stop making fun of me."

"I'm not. Weren't you the first and last kindergarten student at My Dear Watson to demand and receive regular homework assignments?"

"So what of it, Helene? By the time I got to first grade I was reading better than most third graders," Ellenbeth said proudly.

"You're still way ahead, so you can relax a little."

"Yeah. Besides, we *are* learning stuff. What about yesterday, Ellenbeth?" Arthur added. "I know all about space. Isn't that learning?"

"Not *all* about space, Arthur, but you, indeed, have begun to lay a foundation of knowledge."

"Hey, you called me Arthur." Arthur sounded very proud.

"You like that?" asked Kathy.

"Sure. Mr. Fred only calls people by their first names when he thinks they've done something special or good. Haven't you noticed?"

"How come *he* figured that out?" said Lucy, pointing at Arthur.

"How come *you* didn't?" asked Arthur, pointing at Lucy.

"I still don't think any of this 'prove he's an alien junk' has to do with school," Ellenbeth grumbled.

"It has everything to do with school, Miss Maggin. Follow me, class." Goldberg Fred walked into the back room.

It was completely changed. The piles of paper, and buckets of clay, and boxes of fabric, and jars of paint, and glue, and coffee cans filled with Magic Markers, brushes, and scissors, and almost everything else a kid would need to make a picture or a mask or a costume were gone. Where there had been friendly mess, there was now order.

Neatly arranged on the tabletops were rows of books, a box of empty test tubes and glass slides, a computer, two empty aquarium tanks, an overhead projector, a microscope and, pointing out the window, a telescope.

"Wow!" said Mike.

"Yeah," said Paul, heading straight for the microscope.

"Where's our art stuff?" Louise asked.

Goldberg Fred pointed to the shelves along the wall,

where our supplies were easily reachable but out of the way.

"What's all this for?" asked Aaron, picking up an empty test tube.

"Scientific research," said Goldberg Fred, "if you accept my challenge."

"What challenge?" someone asked.

"The Spaceman Challenge," I said.

"The what?"

"We're going to prove that Goldberg Fred—" I began.

"—came from far away to be your teacher, or not," Goldberg Fred finished.

"How?" a bunch of kids yelled.

"You're going to buddy-up. Two students to a team. Each team will pick something to study—which will prove or disprove who I really am. Get it?"

"No."

"How do we know what to study?"

"This is too hard."

"We're only sixth graders."

"There is nothing *only* about sixth graders," said Goldberg Fred.

"Is that an insult?"

"It could be a compliment."

"Perhaps it's simply an observation," said Goldberg Fred. "Are you ready to begin?"

"Begin what?"

"Begin how?"

"I think I understand," said Paul.

"Then explain it to your classmates, Mr. Saladino."

"Look, we all think Goldberg Fred is not—well, not a normal sixth-grade teacher."

"Paul, you think the man's off a spaceship," said Aaron.

"Or out of a time machine," Bettina added.

"Or from another dimension," I said.

"It doesn't matter what I think. It matters what we all think and can prove. For example, we don't really know if he comes from Mars because we don't know much about Mars or what kind of creatures might live there or if Goldberg Fred could be one," said Paul.

"One what, Paul?"

"One of those creatures that might live on Mars if Mars could support life." Paul was losing patience.

"Don't forget Duck, the Frinch Puddle," I said.

"The what?" a couple of kids asked.

"Oh, right," said Paul. "The Frinch Puddle. It's what Goldberg Fred called him. Duck is a Frinch Puddle dog who hunts Puddle Sharks. Duck and Goldberg Fred could be from different planets or different parts of the same planet."

A couple of kids groaned.

"That's the point of all this," Paul continued. "If you

believe this is just a big nothing, help prove it. If you believe Goldberg Fred is a person from another planet, help prove it. Pick a topic—like Mars."

"I want to study Mars," said Kathy.

"I'll work with you, but maybe we should study the three planets closest to Earth," Bettina said.

"Which are those?"

Bettina pointed to a map of the solar system hanging on the wall. "Mercury, Venus, and Mars."

"We'll take Jupiter, Saturn, and Uranus," said Arthur, who was standing next to Louise.

"And Pluto," Louise added.

"Nothing can live on Pluto," said Bettina. "It's too far from the sun."

"You study your planets and we'll study ours," said Louise.

"Exactly," said Goldberg Fred.

The class began to get an idea a minute. Two kids were going to study the Earth to see if Goldberg Fred could have come from an underground cave or the center of the Earth. Two kids chose geography to see if they could find a secret place on Earth where a race of Goldberg Freds could be hiding.

Mike naturally chose space flight. He wanted to build a model of a ship that could fly between planets and star systems. Kids who never said much of anything in class were picking topics to study and partners to study with as fast as they could get the words out of their mouths.

Finally we were down to just a few people. Paul asked if he could study Goldberg Fred and Duck as living beings. He wanted to compare them to humans and Earth dogs. When Goldberg Fred said fine, Paul had a volunteer partner next to him in less than a second. Ellenbeth picked ESP as her subject, and I thought of joining her but got my own idea so fast that it simply popped out of my mouth before I could stop it.

"I would like to find out if you or your kind were ever here before," I said.

"And how might you do that?" asked Goldberg Fred.

"By looking at strange people in history—inventions that maybe didn't fit—ideas that maybe were ahead of their time—places like Stonehenge in England."

"What's Stonehenge?" asked Helene.

"A place where giant stones were set in circles thousands of years ago. Nobody knows how the people back then moved the stones. My mother told me about it," I said.

"History is a long time and a lot of events, Miss Murray. Looking for me in it will be like looking for a needle in a haystack." Goldberg Fred winked at me.

Before I could think of a snappy remark, Helene volunteered to be my research partner.

"One last thing," said Goldberg Fred. "Each team will be responsible for keeping the rest of the class informed about anything they learn. There will be a schedule posted, and each day assigned teams will report to their classmates. At the end of the project, each team will produce a written report—with pictures, diagrams, photographs, or whatever is necessary."

"Necessary for what?"

"Necessary to make your report as clear as possible."

Not a single kid complained. "We're going to get you, Mr. Fred," said Paul cheerfully.

"Find you out."

"Uncover your secret."

"Get you, get you, get you good!"

"Good luck, kiddies. You'll need it. Line up for lunch." Goldberg Fred switched on his tape player to top volume.

We marched out of the room, down the stairs, and finally, into the cafeteria. Everyone was in such a good mood that nobody complained when lunch turned out to be mystery stew, or as we called it, Dear Watson's Revenge.

"Do you think we can really find out who he is?" asked Paul.

"Sure," said Helene.

"Maybe," I said. "He's diabolically clever—a master trickster." A slimy serpent, I thought to myself.

Goldberg Fred looked up from his plate at the end of our table and said loudly, "Worms are slimy, Miss Murray. Slugs and snails are slimy. Slime is slimy. Serpents, generally, are not."

"Yick." "Ugh." "Gross." Some of my classmates were laughing, and some looked a little sick.

"Why did he say that, Anya?" asked Susan, who was sitting at the table next to ours.

"Ask him," I said, trying to figure a way to close off my thoughts.

"Why did you say that, Mr. Fred?"

"Miss Murray called me a slimy snake."

"Serpent," I corrected.

"I didn't hear her say that," said Helene.

"Well, I did." Goldberg Fred and most of the class went back to picking things they recognized as edible out of the stew.

"He did it again, didn't he?" whispered Paul.

"Yes, and you don't have to whisper, do you?"

"You're right. If he can read thoughts, whispering is stupid."

"Maybe if we wear tinfoil on our heads, it will keep our thoughts in," Helene suggested. "Of course, we'll be walking around looking like baked potatoes."

"This is serious, Helene. We could line some hats with foil and see what happens," said Paul.

"And what if the foil works like an antenna on a radio and makes it easier for him to hear our thoughts?" I asked.

Then I turned to Helene, whose sides were shaking with laughter and said, "I don't see what you find so funny? If you don't shut up, I'm going to pour stew down your shirt."

"Temper, temper, wetfoot," Helene gasped. She shoved a piece of bread in her mouth and began chewing furiously.

"Did you hear that?" I said, putting my hands over my ears.

"What?"

"That laughing."

"You mean Helene?" asked Paul.

"I'm not laughing now."

"Then you do hear it, Paul." I pressed my hands tightly against my ears.

"Arrgh," said Paul, covering up his own ears.

"Double arrgh," said Helene, following his example.

We stared at a blank-faced Goldberg Fred, who was calmly shoveling mystery stew into his mouth while he giggled like a maniac inside our heads.

Who Is Goldberg Fred—What Is He?

14

The Spaceman Challenge

T he Spaceman Challenge became the most important thing in our lives. Each day at school was an adventure. We never knew what clue, what piece of information a team might uncover to help us prove that Goldberg Fred and Duck were from some other planet—or time or dimension—or not. We studied and then taught each other subjects many of us couldn't even spell when we began—like parapsychology and geology, geography and astronomy, physiology, and microbiology to name only a few. We made models of solar systems, spaceships, planets, and aliens. We drew maps and graphs and pictures. We learned to separate science fiction from scientific fact.

We became experts at using the reference section in the public library. We sent away for information from just about every government agency in the United States and a few in Canada. We found experts and wrote them letters. Some wrote back and answered our questions. Most amazing of all, we found ourselves thinking and working on the Spaceman Challenge during weekends and holidays. School, that place where we could come, share ideas, and make plans, became the place we wanted to be.

We got used to strange things happening to us, like kids changing their personalities, sometimes suddenly. For example, one day Crazy Arnold stood up in class and announced that his name was Arnold. Period. He told us that from that moment on, he wanted to be thought of as eccentric, artistic, unique, clever, and original—a free sixth-grade spirit. Arthur laughed and said, "You sure can be funny, Crazy Arnie." Arnold put Arthur on the floor using what he said was a martial art technique learned from his older sister.

Nobody was surprised. Something unexpected happened in our classroom almost every day. It was an exciting time for 6-A.

Paul and his project partner, Erica Thompson, formerly the quietest kid in class, decided that in order to thoroughly examine Goldberg Fred and Duck as beings, they had to study their habitat. Each day, dressed in matching trench coats, Erica and Paul tried following man and dog home. Each day they lost the two alien beings at a different place in town.

"Maybe they have a back portal," Helene joked when Paul and Erica finally shared their problem with the class, ". . . and a couple of side portals, not to mention a sliding-glass patio portal and—"

"Not funny, Helene. This is a big clue. The man and so-called dog do not go home to a regular house." Erica passed out copies of a town map she had duplicated in the school office. She and Paul had marked all the places Goldberg Fred and Duck had "disappeared" from sight.

"It doesn't make sense," said Kathy, studying the map. "According to this, their invisible house is as big as the whole downtown."

"Maybe you two are terrible at following people, and they're ditching you," Mike suggested.

"Headline: SPACE SLEUTHS STRIKE OUT," Helene quipped.

"Or: SPACE SLEUTHS TOO SPACEY FOR SURVEIL-LANCE," Alice added.

"Good one," said Helene. "How about—"

"Cut it out, clowns. This is important," I said. "It could be that they go into a spaceship which picks them up when they signal it—like a taxi."

"Or maybe, like Helene said, it's a huge starship that hovers over the whole town, and they go in different doors—depending on where they are," said Kathy.

"I was joking," Helene groaned.

"You can get beamed up from anywhere," said Arthur.

"Beaming up happens on television, not in real life," insisted Lucy.

"We don't know that do we?" said Arthur.

"Arthur's right," I said. "We're investigating a possible spaceman and spacedog—anything might be the truth."

"Have you ever seen them actually disappear?" asked Ellenbeth.

"No," Erica and Paul admitted. "But we're never more than seconds behind them. Isn't that right, Mr. Fred?"

Over the weeks we had learned that Goldberg Fred might choose not to answer a question, but he never lied.

"Mr. Saladino and Miss Thompson are correct. They have been as close as shadows much of the time—to no avail." I could hear Goldberg Fred chuckling inside my head. So could Erica and Paul. I could tell from the expressions on their faces.

"When I leave here each afternoon with Duck, we do our errands and go home."

"But where is that home? What is that home?" Erica lamented. "He's not in the phone book," she said to the class.

"Maybe he has an unlisted number," Ellenbeth suggested.

"Perhaps I have no phone," said Goldberg Fred.

"His file in the school office lists a post-office box number instead of an address," said Paul.

"How did you get to see his file?" I asked.

"We have our ways," said Erica, smoothing the lapels of her trench coat.

"I receive my mail at the post office, as do many people. You've observed me doing so, Mr. Saladino."

"You didn't tell us he receives mail," Alice complained. "That could change everything. Why would a spaceman receive mail?"

"Why not?" said Goldberg Fred.

"It gives a whole new meaning to 'via air mail,' " said Helene. "Actually, it should be 'via airless mail' if it comes through space."

"You're giving a whole new meaning to airhead," I said. "This is serious. If the mail is coming from anywhere on earth—and it has to be if he's getting it at the post office—maybe there are more of them here."

"Them who, Anya? Freds or Ducks?" asked Arnold. "How should I know?"

"More? Like an invasion?" Lucy asked nervously.

"Maybe like an expedition," I said, looking at Goldberg Fred. "As slimy as he is, I can't imagine Goldberg Fred invading someplace."

"Why?" Lucy asked.

"Because invasion means fighting and hurting and killing. Can you see him doing that? The man can be sneaky and mean, but he's not violent," said Alice.

"Ah, praise from the highest source," said Goldberg Fred.

Alice, who hadn't made a weapon in weeks, smiled at Goldberg Fred and said in a soft voice, "We *are* going to get you, Mr. Fred. *Nobody* can beat an entire sixth-grade class—especially this one."

"I hold my breath in anticipation," said Goldberg Fred, taking a deep breath that made his cheeks puff out.

"That's all we have today," said Paul. He whispered something in Erica's ear, and they turned up their collars, stuffed their hands deep into their trenchcoat pockets, and swaggered detective-like to the back of the room.

"They're getting stranger and stranger," said Mike.

"How come they wear those coats whenever they report to us?" asked Alice.

"Maybe someone should start studying the effect of spaceman surveillance on Earth kids," suggested Arnold. "And speaking of surveillance," he continued, "has anyone noticed that Goldberg Fred is still holding his breath?"

"Maybe someone should whack him on the back or something. He's turning bright red," said Mike.

Goldberg Fred's breath kind of exploded out of his

mouth. "That felt good," he said, shaking his head back and forth letting his cheeks flop loosely. Duck shook his head, too, but it looked more normal on a dog.

"It's now time to hear from our imaginative Miss Murray and her comic sidekick, Miss Holman."

Helene and I had been studying history to see if we could find evidence of space people visiting Earth in the past. We had been reporting to the class on incredible inventions and constructions that some people insisted were thought of and built by visitors from space, not humans. We had reported on the great pyramids in Egypt, Stonehenge in England, the enormous rock figures on Easter Island—which is thousands of miles from the nearest continent—the astronomical and mathematical skills of the ancient Mayas in Central America, and a bunch of other things. The problem was that we were coming to a conclusion we didn't want to reach.

"Should we tell them today?" Helene whispered.

"We have to tell them soon so we can do the rest of our project," I said.

"You tell them, Anya."

"No, you."

"Would you please give your report. You're wasting time," Aaron complained.

"Human beings are very smart," I began.

"—and inventive," Helene added.

"We now believe that the advanced thought needed to

invent astronomy and mathematics and navigation," I said.

"—and Stonehenge and the pyramids," Helene added.

"—and all other amazing sciences and constructions on Earth," I continued.

"—came from the brains of human beings," Helene finished.

The class was silent for a minute. Then Alice spoke up. "I don't get it. Are you saying that you think Goldberg Fred and Duck are from Earth?"

"No, we're saying that we can't find any proof that space beings have been here before. The things we researched were invented by people or built by people," Helene answered.

"Prove it," said Paul.

"Right. Mr. Fred said that history is a long time and a lot of events. You couldn't have possibly studied all of history." Lucy sounded smug.

"Don't be stupid, Lucile. Of course we didn't. It wasn't necessary. We're going to begin the second half of our project and prove that humans had the intelligence and skill to build one of the great wonders of the world," I said.

"We're going to show you how people built the pyramids," Helene paused for dramatic effect, "by building one."

A couple of kids laughed, but Helene and I ignored

them and went into the back room to make our plans. After a while, we invited Mike and Alice, the class master builders, to join us. We were going to need some technical advice.

Thanksgiving came and went. It was one week before Christmas vacation. The school was having an open house for parents. Unlike most of the other teachers who liked to see the parents in private, Goldberg Fred invited us to be there—in fact he insisted on it.

We spent a whole day arranging our constructions and models and maps and drawings around the room. Swinging from pulleys, Mike's spaceships could be lowered to eye level. Arthur and Bettina had gotten together with another team and had built a large model of our solar system. It dipped and swayed as it hung low from the center of the ceiling. From each planet and moon hung a neatly printed card describing its atmosphere and what form of life, if any, might be able to live there.

Tables at the back of the room were filled with projects: a volcano that worked, a replica of a cave with an underground lake and the most delicate, beautiful stalactites and stalagmites, and our perfect, miniature pyramid display showing three stages of construction and tiny pipe-cleaner people at work. In every corner, on every wall, on every shelf—in both rooms—our work was on display. On top of each desk sat the notebooks we had been keeping and the reports we had written.

"This is unbelievable," said Paul, tacking up a chart titled *The Terra Eating Habits of a Spaceman and His Dog*.

"Looks like they eat believable stuff to me," said Helene, peering over his shoulder. "Mostly hamburgers, occasionally pizza . . ."

"Very funny, buzzard brain. I meant the work we've done is unbelievable—look around you. Besides, this chart is nothing. I think I've broken the case," Paul bragged.

"What are you talking about?" I demanded.

"Yeah," said Mike. "All information was supposed to be shared. Nothing secret."

Other kids heard our conversation and came over.

"Okay. Okay. I'm sorry. A week ago I got Mr. Fred to let me have a tiny blood sample, a cutting of hair, and a skin scraping. I examined them under the microscope. They didn't seem to have cells that matched the ones in the books—so I sent the microscope slides to NASA." Paul looked proud of himself. Erica looked bugged.

"You didn't tell me," she complained.

"He didn't tell anyone. Paul, you're a creep," I said.

"But *I'm* supposed to be his learning partner."

"Well, it doesn't matter anyway," said Mike. "Paul probably messed up the slides or read them wrong."

"What if he didn't? What if the cells are different?" asked Susan.

"Nobody at NASA is going to pay any attention to a bunch of slides sent by a kid who claims his teacher is a spaceman. They'll throw them away," said Mike confidently.

"YOU'RE WRONG! I didn't mess up the slides. I *did* see different cells and someone important *will* look at them. I'll prove to you I've solved the case. I'll show you now. Can I please have some more samples, Mr. Fred, so I can show them to the class?" he begged.

"No, Paul. The Spaceman Challenge is over. You've all done wonderful work. Your parents will be most proud of you."

"How can the Spaceman Challenge be over? We haven't proven that you're a space person yet," I said.

"And you haven't proven that I am not a space person, Anya. Tomorrow you will weigh all the evidence and come to a conclusion."

"We need more time," I insisted.

"More time."

"Another month or two."

"There will be new and exciting challenges for you to pursue, kiddies. Believe me, tomorrow this particular challenge ends."

Goldberg Fred played some Sousa marches for us while we straightened chairs and made the room perfect for our parents. Our good feelings returned. We left school smiling.

On the way out of the building, I heard Paul telling Erica that he was sure NASA would look at his slides because he had a witness to his discovery.

"I sent a set of specimen slides to my Uncle Pat."

"So what?" said Erica.

"So my uncle's an FBI agent and I'm his favorite nephew. The FBI has its own laboratory—he'll have someone look at the slides and then he'll call NASA."

"You had better be wrong, Paul," I snarled in his ear.

"What?" Paul looked totally surprised.

"You had better hope your uncle doesn't pay attention to what you sent him," Arthur warned.

"What are you talking about?" Paul looked from Arthur to me and back again. "I thought the whole point of the challenge was to prove Goldberg Fred and Duck are aliens."

"What's going on?" Helene asked.

I explained as others joined us. The entire class surrounded Paul in the playground.

"Hey, leave me alone. I just wanted experts to confirm my evidence," Paul said.

"You turned him in," said Alice.

"*You* hate him, Alice. You were building weapons to destroy him," said Paul.

"I was trying to outwit him. Now I don't care. I just want to know how he got here with Duck. Goldberg Fred is *our* spaceman. You stink, Paul."

"They're going to come and arrest him," I said.

"My uncle wouldn't do that."

"Hah!" I said.

"There's a good chance his uncle won't even look at the slides," said Kathy.

"He will. I called him two nights ago. His friend is a biologist at the laboratory. . . ." Paul's voice trailed off into a kind of whimper.

"Maybe the slides will break on the way to Washington," Aaron said.

"My uncle said they arrived safely," Paul whispered.

"Maybe Mr. Fred gave Paul a sample of someone else's hair and blood."

"He did not," Paul insisted.

"What if none of this matters because Mr. Fred is just a weird Earthling—with a few extrasensory abilities," Ellenbeth said hopefully.

"He is not!" Paul shouted.

"Go soak your head, Paul," I said. We left him standing alone on the playground, trying to figure out why the entire class had turned on him.

"I think that I was so busy learning stuff that I didn't notice something important," I confided to Helene.

"What?"

"Goldberg Fred is a very good teacher."

"That's not what you were going to say," said Helene.

"How do you know?"

"I know."

"Then what was I going to say?"

"You like him."

"Who?"

"You. Goldberg Fred."

"Oh, him."

"Anya—"

"No way. He's impossible."

"So are you."

"Maybe I am. Maybe I even like him. Do you like him?" I asked.

"Everyone in the class does, even if they won't admit it."

"Helene, I just thought of something. We should warn him about Paul's uncle."

"How? He has no phone."

"He telephoned us when we found Duck."

"Well, then his number is unlisted, or he called from a phone booth."

"We can't go knock on his door because nobody knows where he lives."

"Or where his portal is."

"Very funny. We'll tell him tonight at the open house."

"I hope we're not too late."

"Me, too."

The Open House

15

My mother and I arrived at school at seven o'clock that night. As we passed the other classrooms, we could see the usual Christmas stuff glued to the windows and the usual classroom stuff pinned to the walls. In each room, a handful of parents were sitting on kid-sized chairs or on desktops, looking uncomfortable. No kids were around.

We were almost at our private attic landing when we heard the music.

"Doesn't sound much like a Christmas carol." My mother gasped and staggered up the last few steps.

"It's 'The Stars and Stripes Forever' by John Philip

Sousa. He lived from 1854 to 1932. Mr. Fred is a fan."
I explained to my mother, who had turned a funny green-
ish grey color and was not breathing properly.

"Mister?" she wheezed. "That's a first for you." She
leaned against the nearest wall. "What ever happened to
Slimy Fred?"

"An educated person has an open mind," I said.

"Will wonders never cease," my mother coughed.

"You should start an exercise program, Mom. You're
in lousy shape."

"Thanks. I'll be sure to put it on my list," my mother
gasped, "right between clean out the attic and paint the
living room."

"Your green color is going away." I was relieved.

"I was green?"

"Sort of grey-green."

"I don't know how Mr. Fred goes up and down these
stairs all day long." My mother pushed herself away from
the wall and took off her coat.

"He only has to go up two or three times most days.
Down is easy," I said.

"I'm looking forward to down," said my mother and
walked into my classroom.

Goldberg Fred's desk was covered with plates of cook-
ies and cupcakes and stacks of paper cups which surrounded a huge bowl filled with pink liquid and ice. My
classmates were standing around the desk. No one was

eating. No one was drinking. Duck was curled up in Goldberg Fred's chair, sleeping.

"Uh-oh," I whispered to Helene.

"I know," said Helene. "The last time a teacher made a party for us, it was the end. No one wants to eat."

"Did you warn Mr. Fred?"

"*Mister?*" said Alice. "*You* called him mister?"

"Big deal."

I view it as a big deal. Thank you, said Goldberg Fred inside my head.

I closed my eyes and tried to send a warning thought to Goldberg Fred, who was across the room.

"What are you doing?" asked Mike.

"Trying to telepathically warn Mr. Fred about Paul's uncle."

"Anya called Fred 'mister,' " Arthur announced.

"Would everyone stop making such a big deal about it," I said, closing my eyes again.

"Why don't you just go over and tell him what you want to tell him," Mike suggested.

"I don't want any adults to overhear."

"I think it worked; open your eyes," said Helene.

A smiling Goldberg Fred made his way over to us. "The message has been received, kiddies. We from space—or not—thank you for your concern. Eat, drink, and be merry . . ." Goldberg Fred moved into the crowd of parents who were circling the room.

"Oh no," said Ellenbeth.

"Oh no?" I asked.

"For tomorrow we die," she muttered.

"What?"

"It's a quote. 'Eat, drink, and be merry, for tomorrow we die,' " Ellenbeth explained.

"He was joking," said Helene, grabbing a cupcake nervously.

"Maybe," said Alice, biting into a cookie. "Maybe not."

"Then why are you all eating?" I asked, watching as the rest of my classmates began stuffing their faces.

"What else is there to do?" Arthur spewed crumbs into the air.

"Don't talk with your mouth full," I said.

"Look at our parents," said Aaron, changing the topic.

"Why?" asked Kathy, pouring herself a glass of punch.

"Just look."

We had been so busy talking to each other that we hadn't noticed the effect the roomful of our work was having on our parents. They were moving slowly from project to project, wall to wall, room to room. Some of the parents had expressions of shock and amazement on their faces. Some were smiling. A few were rooted in front of particular pieces of work. My mother was stroking one of the pyramids as if it were a cat.

"I bet I get a raise in my allowance," said Aaron.

"Look, my parents like my extra-credit project," said

Alice, pointing to the two people bent over in front of a little model she had built of the Hubble Space Telescope. "The real telescope had design flaws. My model is perfect."

"How can you get extra credit when in this class there is *no* credit?" asked Arnold.

"There *is* credit. There are just no grades," explained Alice.

"But how can you tell?" asked Arnold.

"Tell what?"

"Tell what's extra."

"You're giving me a headache," said Alice.

"I think we hypnotized our parents," I said.

"We certainly surprised them," said Ellenbeth.

The last family to arrive were the Saladinos. "Are you still mad at me?" Paul asked.

"Did you call your uncle and tell him that the slides were a joke?" I asked.

"No."

"Then we're still mad."

"I don't understand any of you," said Paul.

"Think about it, Paul. You'll figure it out," I said and turned my back on him.

Our parents spent a long time looking at our work. At eight o'clock, Goldberg Fred turned off the march music and asked everyone to come into the front classroom. It was pretty crowded. We had set a school record for attendance on parents' night—one hundred percent.

"Students—on the floor here." Goldberg Fred gestured to the floor near the chalkboard. As many adults as possible sat at our desks. The rest stood along the walls.

Goldberg Fred looked out at the room of smiling adults and spoke. "The students in this class believe I am not from around here. These projects you see and, in fact, most of the teaching and all of the learning accomplished this term have been the direct work of the students, in a collective effort to discover where exactly I, and my furry friend Duck, are from."

"I don't understand," said someone. "Why would they get involved with all of this just to find out if you're from New Jersey or Mississippi—or Canada, for that matter?"

We began giggling. Goldberg Fred smiled one of his worst smiles at us. We shut up. Our parents looked at Goldberg Fred with admiration.

"I'll let a student explain. Any volunteers?" Goldberg Fred nodded at Paul. Paul stood up.

"We think—no, we *know*—that Mr. Fred and his supposed dog Duck are from another planet—or time—or dimension." Paul's parents both covered their faces with their hands.

Paul continued. "We call our research project the Spaceman Challenge. Its goal is to find out where they might be from and how they got here."

Some of the parents were laughing out loud. Goldberg Fred winked at them. A number winked back.

"We're serious. We don't care if you believe us now. You'll believe when you see our proof—*my* proof!" Paul shouted.

Goldberg Fred patted Paul on the shoulder and sort of pressed down on him until he was sitting on the floor with the rest of us. "If any of you parents have questions or comments about the Spaceman Challenge or about the individual research and reports your children have done, please feel free to speak now."

"Personally, I don't care how you got them to do it. This work is great—remarkable for a sixth-grade class," said a father.

"Especially *this* sixth-grade class," added a mother. All the parents nodded their heads as they remembered the first weeks of school.

"It's amazing what you've done with them in a little over two months."

"They've done it themselves," said Goldberg Fred. "All they needed was a reason to unlock their own minds."

"And you gave it to them!"

"I think they provided it for themselves."

"Would all this have happened if you hadn't been here?"

"Perhaps not," said a modest Goldberg Fred.

"What a guy." Parents were on their feet shaking Goldberg Fred's hand and pounding him on the back. There wasn't a single complaint or even a single "How's my kid doing?" Everyone in 6-A was doing great.

While the parents were having a love fit for Goldberg Fred, we kids stood around finishing off the pink punch.

"Tomorrow's the big day," said Mike.

"Do you think we'll prove they're from space?" asked Alice.

"At least we'll prove that they're not from around here," said Helene.

"You know, I don't think we'll prove anything definite," I said.

"I do," said Paul.

"Look, you don't have a scrap of evidence to show us," said Alice.

"Right, you sent your alleged slides to your uncle," said Erica.

"They're not alleged, they're real slides—" Paul began.

Ellenbeth interrupted. "We have lots of speculation—"

"And theories—" added Kathy.

"And possibilities," I finished.

"We'll just have to spend next term getting more evidence," said Helene happily.

"But I *have* the proof," Paul insisted. "Goldberg Fred and Duck are not from Earth. I broke the case!"

"You know, it doesn't matter to me where Goldberg Fred and Duck are from."

"What are you talking about, Anya?" Paul demanded.

"She's right. I don't care if they're from Brooklyn."

"Or Ohio."

"Or Arizona."

"Or Texas."

"I like Goldberg Fred," I said.

"Did I hear you right?"

"You heard me. He's the weirdest person I have ever met in my life, but so what?"

"I agree with that thought," said Arnold.

"Don't you mind that he makes fun of us and calls us names, Anya?"

"We make fun of him and call him names."

"I love Duck."

I love you, too. And I love old, slimy Goldberg Fred, a voice screeched inside our heads. It was so loud that a number of my classmates looked stunned.

"Was that Goldberg Fred?" asked Helene, shaking her head as if trying to clear her brain.

Guess again! the silent voice filled our brains.

"I think it's Duck," I said. Duck winked at me.

"What's Duck?" asked my mother, joining our group.

"Nothing, Mom."

"He's grown a great deal," said my mother, scratching Duck behind the ears.

"Tripled in size since October," said Paul, zipping up his jacket.

"Puppies are amazing," said my mother. "I would have liked to keep him."

"I don't think so, Mrs. Murray," said Helene.

"Why? Oh, yes. I see. You think he's a Martian or something." My mother wrapped her scarf around her face to cover up the fact that she was starting to laugh at us.

"You're not subtle, Mother," I said to her back as she guffawed her way out of the room.

"It's 6-A against a disbelieving world," said Helene.

"I hope it stays that way," I said.

All my classmates, except Paul of course, nodded their heads in agreement.

Good-bye, Mr. Fred

The next morning I woke up long before my alarm went off. I was dressed and eating my breakfast before my mother finished her shower.

"What's the hurry?" my mother asked. She poured herself a cup of coffee, sat down at the table, plugged in her hair dryer, unfolded the morning newspaper, and got set to do her usual three things at once—four, if you count talking to me.

"I don't know," I said, and I didn't.

"I do. You're still excited about last night. It was probably the best school open house I will ever attend. I'm enormously proud of you, Anya." My mother put down the dryer and the coffee cup, leaned over, and hugged me.

I was so happy on the way to school that I didn't notice it had begun to snow until Arthur caught up to me.

"You're the only kid I know who wears rain boots on sunny days and no boots in the snow. Is it some alien thing, Anya? Are you really Anya Murray, Spacegirl?"

"Everyone's a comedian," I complained as Helene joined us at the corner. I realized for the first time that my feet were pretty cold.

"The world would be a better place if that were true," said Helene.

"Serious isn't bad, Helene."

"Funny is better."

We arrived at the playground a half hour early. So did the rest of the class. Goldberg Fred was nowhere in sight.

"Where is he?" asked Mike, shifting from foot to foot to keep warm.

"It's early," I said.

"Maybe he doesn't want to catch pneumonia by standing around in the freezing cold." Kathy's teeth chattered as she spoke.

"Why aren't they letting us into the gym?" Lucy complained.

"It's too early. We're the only kids here," said Kathy.

"Why are we here so early?" asked Helene.

"Is that a trick question?" asked Arthur.

"Yes."

"Goldberg Fred's always early," said Aaron.

"Maybe he's gone away. He gave us a party last night," said Alice glumly.

"And we ate. We shouldn't have eaten anything. It was a jinx," Lucy lamented.

"Don't be ridiculous," I said. "It wasn't a party, it was an open house. Besides, Duck is here."

"Where?" asked Arnold.

"Over here, next to my leg, trying to work his head under my jacket. Goldberg Fred wouldn't leave without Duck."

"Why?"

"Because he probably loves Duck—they're a team— an alien and his dog."

"That's an answer to the wrong why. Why does Duck have his head under your jacket?"

My ears are cold, Duck telepathed loudly.

I pulled my jacket collar away from my neck and slipped it over my chin and mouth so I could speak directly to the Frinch Puddle. "Duck, can't you do that in a softer way? I think you're starting to injure our brain cells."

I'll try, Duck's thoughts bounced around in my head.

"How come he's talking in English?" Mike groaned painfully.

"He's not talking, he's telepathing," Ellenbeth corrected.

"Well, it's in English. Mr. Fred said Duck was from Frence. Shouldn't he be telepathing in French?"

Oh, such confusion. They speak French in France. In Frence, we speak Franch—F-R-A-N-C-H. Here in the U.S.A., I speak English. I am a bilingual Frinch Puddle.

"You're a bilingual Frinch headache," Helene moaned.

"It feels like someone just squeezed my brain." Susan took off her hat.

"Since he seems to know how to spell, maybe we should teach Duck to write," I said, rubbing my forehead.

"By the way, Anya, exactly when did Duck get here?" asked Alice. "Did he come with Mr. Fred?"

"How do I know? I'm just a dog tent," I complained.

"Did you see him arrive?" asked Paul.

"Why should I tell you?"

"You didn't, did you, Anya? He just appeared—out of thin air." Paul was getting excited.

"If he did, then maybe he's a ghost. Why don't you call your uncle and tell him we have a telepathic ghost dog haunting us," I said.

"A space spirit with extrasensory powers," said Helene.

"A space specter," Ellenbeth added.

"Make your uncle think it was all a joke," said Mike.

"If you do that, Paul, we'll forgive you for being a quisling," I offered.

The bell rang before Paul could answer.

"It's too early for the bell," said Alice.

"Who cares? It's saving our lives." My feet had turned into two blocks of ice.

"Gym repairs going on. Proceed directly to your classrooms." The teachers at the double doors waved us into the building.

We rushed forward. Duck stumbled beside me, his head stuffed under my jacket. The teachers were so busy sorting out kids that they didn't notice the four gigantic dog feet skidding beside me on the slippery floor. Goldberg Fred was waiting for us in our classroom.

"Where were you?" I asked.

"There, and now here."

A steaming cup of hot chocolate sat in the middle of each desk.

"Uh-oh, more food," Lucy moaned.

As we settled into our seats, Goldberg Fred and Duck made themselves comfortable on Goldberg Fred's desktop. "Well, Earth kiddies, it's time to say good-bye." For the first time since we met him, Goldberg Fred looked sad.

"Where are you going?" My breakfast turned into a great weight in my stomach.

"Far away."

Duck sighed.

"But we haven't finished the Spaceman Challenge," said Paul.

"Learning isn't a race. There is no finish line you can cross. Besides, the possibilities of the Challenge are endless. It can't be finished. It shouldn't be finished."

"I don't understand," said Arthur.

"I thought the Spaceman Challenge was finding out if you were an alien," said Kathy.

"I tricked you." Goldberg Fred smiled.

"It figures," I said. I could feel tears beginning to fill my eyes.

"But you *are* an alien, aren't you?" Mike asked.

"I am not from around here." Goldberg Fred laughed as he wiggled his long fingers in the direction of the windows.

"I told you. We shouldn't have eaten at the party," Lucy wailed.

"There was no cause and effect regarding the refreshments, Lucile—just coincidence. Now it's time for all of you to use your excellent minds to their fullest capacities. This morning we will reason together and compare the results of your hard work. Why don't you begin, Anya. What are your conclusions about us?"

"I think that Duck is definitely not from around here."

"And me?"

"You, too."

"But where is the proof?"

"You're telepathic," I said.

"Am I? How can you prove it?"

I looked around the room for support. "We've all heard you," said Mike.

"Heard me?"

"Whatever it is a person does when someone is talking inside a person's head." Mike was getting confused.

"Did any of you tape-record my messages?" Goldberg Fred got off the desk and took a slick-looking camera out of his briefcase.

"How can you tape-record telepathy when it doesn't make any actual noise?" I asked.

"Exactly. No proof."

"He's teasing us," Helene said. "He's a very funny man."

"Twisted but funny," whispered Alice.

"He's not a man; he's a space alien," said Paul.

"You disappear through portals," said Erica to Goldberg Fred.

"Guesswork. You've never actually seen me disappear, have you—or gotten photographic proof?" Goldberg Fred snapped Erica's picture.

"Photographing someone who has just disappeared is like tape-recording telepathy—impossible," said Helene.

"Good point, but the fact remains—you have no proof

that I am a visitor from a planet other than Earth." Goldberg Fred leaned over, wiped a smudge of dirt from the tip of Helene's nose, and pointed his camera at her.

"You have a telepathic dog," said Ellenbeth.

"Ah, you finally believe in telepathy. That's nice. Smile." Ellenbeth smiled as Goldberg Fred took her picture. He lowered his camera. "To answer your unspoken question, Ellenbeth, no, I do not pick up all thoughts at all times. That would be like living in a locked room with the sounds of hundreds of radio stations playing nonstop—at the same time—with no off knob. In order to receive, I have to focus."

"That's proof right there," said Ellenbeth. "You read my mind."

"Are you contending that only off-world natives are telepathic?" asked Goldberg Fred.

"Off-world natives?" said Arthur.

"Aliens, space invaders, travelers, intergalactic life forms, Martians—whatever term you pick to describe intelligent beings from other planets," said Goldberg Fred.

"Are you able to receive all of our thoughts at once if you want to?" I asked.

"Yes, but it's wasted effort—sorting out who is thinking what. However, it's no trouble at all for me to transmit thoughts to all of you at the same time. What I do is widen my mental beam."

"He's admitting all of this. Why?" asked Mike.

"I don't know, but it worries me." I had a funny feeling that something was about to go terribly wrong.

"I'm simply admitting I'm a telepath—I have ESP—I'm unusual," said Goldberg Fred.

"I'm taking notes," said Alice, who was writing furiously in the class log.

"We should be tape-recording his confession so they'll believe us," said Paul.

"So *who* will believe us, Paul? We know who Goldberg Fred is, sort of. He's almost telling us. Why do you want taped proof?" I asked.

"I think it's time for us to go home," said Goldberg Fred.

"But we practically just got here," said Arnold, finishing his hot chocolate.

"By *us*, I mean Duck and me."

"Where's home exactly?" asked Helene with a slightly shaky voice.

"A distance from here—quite a distance."

"Why do you have to go now?" I asked.

"I think I can guess. Right, Paul?" Erica was very upset. "Why do you need a tape recording? Want to give it to your uncle, maybe? Is there a reward for turning in off-world citizens?"

"I like that—off-world citizens," Goldberg Fred spoke to Duck, who nodded his head.

The class ignored them and stared at Paul.

"Have you turned into an alien bounty hunter?" Louise asked.

"No," Paul insisted. "I just wanted to tape-record him for my project—my research."

"And I'm the Queen of England," said Helene.

"Mr. Fred, how about Duck?" Arthur asked.

"What about Duck?" said Mr. Fred.

What about me! Duck yelled into our brains.

"Why are you so loud?" asked Arthur.

Me, loud? How can telepathy be loud if it has no sound? Duck's silent voice shrieked. We grabbed our ears which, of course, did no good at all.

"I don't know how, it just is—or seems to be." Arthur looked like he could use an aspirin.

"Duck can't help it, he's Frinch, and all Frinchoids are naturally loud telepaths. It would be easier on your brains if you learned to understand spoken Franch, but there's no time for it now." Goldberg Fred walked to the door and wedged his desk chair under the doorknob.

"Why'd you do that?" asked Mike.

"It's against the fire laws," said Alice.

"Mr. Fred—" I began.

"At this point, you might as well drop all formalities and call me Goldberg," he interrupted. Then Goldberg Fred began moving around the room snapping pictures like crazy. He took one of each of us and many of the work we had done. "Follow me," he said and ran into the back room.

There he arranged us around the books and laboratory equipment and computers. Goldberg Fred took about ten photos of us from different angles and finally set the camera on a table, pushed a switch, and ran to join us. As soon as he was in place, the camera whirred and clicked.

"None of these are going to come out," said Kathy. "You went past thirty-six photos a while back, and you haven't changed your film."

"No need to. This takes a hundred and fifty images per cartridge."

It was then that we noticed Goldberg Fred's camera looked like nothing any of us had ever seen.

"PROOF!" Paul screamed, diving for the camera.

"Proof of what?" asked Goldberg Fred.

"That you're from space—or another time—or dimension." Paul was examining the strange camera.

"I thought we had decided to forget about the time travel and the dimension stuff," said Mike.

"*You* forgot about them, I didn't." Paul was clutching the camera to his chest. "This is my proof."

"Please give me that," said Goldberg Fred. "It breaks easily."

"Give the man his camera," I said.

Duck muttered and yowled.

"What did he say?" I asked.

I said it's not a camera! Duck silently yelled.

Be quiet, Duck, telepathed Mr. Fred.

What does it matter now? Duck's telepathic message shook our brains. *It's over. Our goose is cooked. The game is up. Spill the beans.*

Be quiet because you're beginning to make my *head sore. Spilling the beans is what I was doing.*

"Wow! Did you all hear that?" said Mike. "A telepathic conversation between two off-world citizens."

"Hear it? Are you kidding?" said Helene, holding her head.

"They must have both had their wide beams turned on," I said.

"All Duck has is a wide beam. Fine focusing of thought is not a talent found in his species. To the point . . . this isn't a camera, it's a . . ." Goldberg Fred made a bunch of gurgling and choking noises.

"Are you all right?" I asked, ready to pound him on the back.

"Perfectly, why?"

"You were choking."

"I was merely telling you what this instrument is called in the language of its inventors."

"Could you translate it into English for us?" I asked.

Goldberg Fred grinned. "I guess you could say it's something like a camera, only more so."

"How more?" I asked.

"It records three-dimensional images—moving or still—and the sounds and smells surrounding the images."

"Why—" I began.

"To show to my class back home. I told you I was a teacher. We have to hurry now." Goldberg Fred ran into the front room with Duck at his heels. We followed. As they reached the desk where Goldberg Fred stuffed the camera-like thing into his briefcase, something threw itself against the barricaded door.

"They're here," said Goldberg Fred cheerfully.

"What's here? What's trying to get in?"

"Not green-skinned monsters, Anya. Just some government people," said Goldberg Fred.

"Whose government?"

"Yours, a couple of others. It appears to be a cooperative effort."

"What is?"

"Catching us. Now stand back, they're about to use a battering ram," Goldberg Fred instructed as the door cracked off its hinges and ten people—some in coveralls and some in suits—rushed into the room. Guns drawn, they surrounded Goldberg Fred and Duck.

"Don't shoot them," I yelled. Suddenly all my classmates were screaming and crying.

Old Bad Breath Pomeroy rushed into the room and

tried shouting over our voices. I think he was telling us to calm down. We didn't. It was horrible. There was nothing we could do to help Goldberg Fred and Duck. They were going to be hauled off and examined—locked up—maybe dissected like animals. Our screaming got louder.

Enough, little Earthlings. Goldberg Fred's voice sort of whispered through our heads. *Be silent. Nobody will hurt us if you help.* No class in any school anywhere ever got as quiet as fast as we did.

"What's going on?" asked one of the men in coveralls, looking around nervously.

"I simply got them to put a sock in it," Pomeroy bragged. "I am their principal. Are you going to get that public enemy out of here now?"

"He's not a public enemy, he's . . . well, it's none of your business," said a man in a dark suit.

"Whatever he is, remove him," ordered Pomeroy, "and his flea-bitten mutt."

Nobody listened to Old Bad Breath. The government people stood silently in a tight circle around Goldberg Fred and Duck.

Are you ready to help us? Goldberg Fred telepathed.

Yes, we all thought.

Why can't *they* hear you? I thought.

I don't want them to. Focusing thought is one of the greatest skills—and one of the most useful. Right, Duck?

Right! Everyone, including the government people, flinched.

A plan is beginning to take shape. How nice, Goldberg Fred telepathed.

Where? I thought.

Inside my magnificent brain, of course.

While we waited silently for Goldberg Fred to tell us more, a man in a suit walked into the room. He was talking into a two-way radio. He seemed to be in charge of things.

"Uncle Pat!" said Paul.

"Who else would it be?" I mumbled.

"What are you going to do with them?" Paul asked.

"Thanks for the tip-off, kid, but this is now a matter of national security," said Paul's Uncle Pat. "You've done your job, now let us do ours."

"My job?"

"Sure, kid. There'll probably be a medal in it for you. Maybe even a reward. We knew these bozos were somewhere on Earth. Who knows how long it would have taken us to find them without your help."

"Yeah, who knows," Arthur snarled.

Paul moaned and buried his face in his arms.

"Nice work, rat dung," I said to Paul.

Prisoners 17

QUISLING! BENEDICT ARNOLD! KLINGON! ROMU-
LON! TRAITOR!" Alice hissed at Paul. She made a note
in the log before rummaging in her desk frantically.

No, Alice! Duck was in all our heads. *No violence.*

"Sit on your hands," I begged my classmates. Some
kids twitched as Duck spoke to us, but nobody reached
for an ear or head. The adults in the room didn't seem
to hear Duck. As far as the FBI and Old Bad Breath
knew, we were just a normal class of squirming, twitch-
ing sixth graders.

Why didn't they hear Duck? I thought.

I blocked his thought waves, as I did when your parents

were here. I'm a very talented telepath. Goldberg Fred smiled at us.

"Why are they just standing there?" whispered Helene. "Why don't they take Goldberg and Duck away?"

"You want them to go?"

"No. It's just strange that they aren't moving."

"Remember what happened the last time we tried to move these two," warned Paul's Uncle Pat. The government people were acting as if we weren't there.

"Last time?" said Mike.

"Shhhh," I said.

"They disappeared into thin air," said another man.

"Took all this time to trace them," said a third.

"Trace them? They didn't trace them," complained Bettina. "*Someone* turned them in."

"Shhhh. Just listen," I said.

Right, Anya. One learns by observing and listening. Goldberg Fred's thoughts were light and cheerful as they tickled my brain.

How can you be so calm? I thought.

Who's calm? telepathed Duck.

"We'll keep them surrounded. Last time we let them wander off," said Uncle Pat.

"They were only about fifteen feet from us."

"It was enough. We will begin moving them slowly toward the door. Lock arms. Keep the circle tight. Don't give them room to maneuver. Don't touch them. You know what they can do if you touch them," said Uncle Pat.

What can they do? I thought. I remembered carrying Duck home and drying him off and holding him on my lap.

I love you, the Frinch Puddle hollered in my head.

I love you, too, I thought and noticed that my classmates were nodding and smiling at Duck who was peering out between the legs of a man in coveralls.

Goldberg Fred interrupted. *Here are my plans for the escape. . . .* His instructions were short and to the point.

As a group we began to cry. We wailed, we sobbed, we forced giant salty tears out of our eyes.

"What's going on here?" shouted Uncle Pat.

"All this is too much for them," said Pomeroy.

"They shouldn't be here. Get them out."

Pomeroy gestured for us to stand and follow him. We did—around our surrounded space friends, down the first flight of stairs and down the second flight of stairs. On the ground floor, Pomeroy turned right toward the cafeteria, and we turned left and ran for the door to the playground. "Stop!" he shouted. We ignored him.

On the playground was a semicircle of grey sedans and vans. A tough-looking person stood next to each car. We followed Goldberg Fred's directions exactly. We lined ourselves up on either side of the door, making a corridor.

The government people and their prisoners would have to walk between us.

"GET INSIDE NOW—YOU'LL CATCH PNEUMONIA!" Mr. Pomeroy stood in the doorway shouting.

"Get out of here, kids." A woman in a uniform came running toward us. "You have to move. Go back into the school."

We looked around as if she were talking to some other kids. "Enough of this fooling around. Move!" ordered a man. He grabbed Alice's arm. She bit him on the hand. Before the man could react, the double doors of the school were bashed wide open, and Mr. Pomeroy was shoved aside. The escorts, arms linked in a tight circle, inched through the doorway.

"I'm freezing," Bettina whispered. We had left our coats in the classroom.

Think warm. Goldberg Fred's words seemed to race from my mind into my body, heating every cell. I was suddenly warm as toast. My classmates looked surprised as they stopped shivering. *Neat trick, isn't it?* I could feel Goldberg Fred's chuckles tumble around my brain.

"What are these kids doing here?" shouted Uncle Pat.

"We were just getting rid of them when you showed up."

"Forget them for now. The prisoners are cooperating. We're moving faster than we expected," said Uncle Pat. "Let's get this show on the road."

Shift just a little to the left, said Goldberg Fred to our waiting minds. *The center of your corridor has to face the big tree.* We moved a couple of steps to the left, straightened our lines, and joined hands. Nobody noticed. All adult eyes were riveted on the dangerous Goldberg Fred and Duck.

Thanks, Earth buddies, said Goldberg Fred. *You've done a perfect job.* Goldberg Fred, Duck, and the circle of ten guards slowly shuffled in the only direction possible—between the two rows of kids from 6-A.

"What's wrong? Pick up the pace," ordered Paul's Uncle Pat.

"The aliens are dragging their feet."

"What's the difference? They can't go anywhere. We've got them trapped."

"Want to bet?" whispered Helene.

As the confident circle reached the end of our corridor, Goldberg Fred dropped his briefcase.

This is it, I thought.

I certainly hope so, telepathed Goldberg Fred.

Up, Up, and Away

oldberg Fred bent over to retrieve his briefcase.
Now, Earth kiddies. Do your thing. The message was soft
and friendly—as if the telepathic space citizen were in
no hurry at all. But we knew the truth.

As per Goldberg Fred's instructions, we did what kids,
and especially sixth graders, do better than anyone—we
screamed and screeched at the top of our lungs.

This broke the concentration of the guards and gave
Goldberg Fred enough time to do what he had to do.
He half-straightened up and tossed his briefcase into the
air. It disappeared. Almost at the same moment, Duck,
using Goldberg Fred's back as a ramp, ran up Goldberg
Fred's body, leaped, and, at a spot just over Goldberg

Fred's head, disappeared. Finally, in less time than it takes to tell this, Goldberg Fred reached up, grabbed something we couldn't see, and began hauling himself into what looked like thin air. His hands disappeared, his lower arms disappeared, his head disappeared; he was gone from his waist up.

A guard in coveralls threw herself at Goldberg Fred's legs and grabbed them. Another one, a man in a suit, grabbed onto the woman.

I was sure Goldberg Fred would come popping out of his portal. I was wrong. Someone or something must have been helping him, because all of a sudden Goldberg Fred's legs and the two guards attached to them were yanked toward the invisible door. The guards screamed. As they bumped toward the spaceship, the woman, desperately hanging on to Goldberg Fred's legs, followed him through the portal. The man, suddenly seeing his arms ending in nothingness as his hands were dragged into the portal, screamed one final bloodcurdling scream, let go, and fell to the ground.

By this time, a number of the people in the playground had drawn their weapons and were aiming at the empty air.

"Don't shoot," ordered Uncle Pat. "Dr. English is somewhere up there with the aliens."

"We saw it. We saw them go through a portal." Paul was jumping up and down with happiness.

"Thanks to you, that's the last we'll ever see of them."

"I didn't think they'd come after Mr. Fred," said Paul. "I just wanted to prove he was a spaceman. Honest, Anya. Honest."

"What exactly did you think they'd do, Paul?" I asked.

"He didn't think, period," said Bettina.

"Don't be angry at Paul; he's going to be a fine scientist someday." Goldberg Fred's voice floated through the empty air. In the confusion, the government people didn't seem to notice.

"WHERE ARE YOU?" I shouted.

"In our home away from home, but soon we'll be on our way to our actual home. We want to be there for the holidays."

"ARE YOUR HOLIDAYS THE SAME AS OUR HOLIDAYS?" Alice hollered into the air.

"Similar. Which reminds me . . . please give my holiday greetings to your families." There was a pause, and the woman in coveralls popped into existence at a spot several feet from where the guns were still pointed. She landed on her feet, looking a little confused. She was immediately surrounded and hustled off to one of the vans.

"Where are you from, Mr. Fred?" I asked for the last time.

"Not from around here," answered Goldberg Fred, "and please call me Goldberg."

*

"Couldn't you be a little more specific?" asked Mike.

"Maybe some other time."

"Are you coming back?" I asked.

"If I can work it out with my school board," said Goldberg Fred.

"Is he kidding?" asked Ellenbeth.

"Who knows? He's as slimy and tricky as ever, right, Goldberg?" I said.

"Right, Anya."

"Why are you talking to us and not telepathing?"

"I'm giving my brain a rest."

"Who are you kids talking to?" asked Uncle Pat. The mob of government alien-chasers had gotten over their shock and looked angry enough to throw us in jail.

"Me, they're talking to me!" Goldberg Fred's head popped out of nowhere about fifteen feet in the air.

"Get him!" ordered Uncle Pat.

"How, sir?" asked a man in a suit.

"Get a ladder or something."

"Good-bye, Earthfolk, it's been interesting!"

There was a sound like a door slamming.

"I think Mr. Fred just closed the portal," I said.

Think of me as Goldberg, your friend. The thought was so delicate I almost missed it.

"GOOD-BYE, GOLDBERG. GOOD-BYE, DUCK," I shouted.

GOOD-BYE, EARTH KIDS. I'LL MISS YOU!

"If you come back," Helene said, holding her head, "I am definitely going to learn to speak Franch."

A loud whooshing noise took our minds off our telepathic headaches. A strong wind whirled around the playground, whipping up snow and forcing us to close our eyes. When it stopped, we stared at the sky, trying to see Goldberg Fred's ship.

"They'll be back," said Uncle Pat.

"I hope so," I said.

"I would love to know what the ship looks like," said Alice.

"And what powers it," said Mike.

"And how far it came."

"And where it came from."

"And what makes it invisible."

"And how he moves it around."

"And how the portals work."

"And if Duck and Goldberg Fred are from the same planet."

"Or solar system."

"Or galaxy, even."

"Was Duck a puppy when he arrived here?"

"Was he born in space?"

"Maybe his mother was on the ship."

"Do you think they'll really come back?"

We were interrupted then by the crowd of angry adults.

"You children have to come with us," one of them ordered.

"What are you talking about?" Mr. Pomeroy stepped in front of us.

"We have to debrief them. They've spent weeks with this alien. They may know something. Besides they have to be examined and tested to see if they've been contaminated."

"Ridiculous. These are sixth graders, not spies or criminals, and they look perfectly healthy to me. Any of you children feel sick?" Mr. Pomeroy glared at us. We shook our heads.

"We didn't say they were spies or criminals. This is government business. You have no right to interfere. Step aside."

I spoke up. "Which government? Which branch of government? We want to see your identification."

A couple of people produced little plastic cases with official-looking cards in them. "What's the point, Miss Murray?" Pomeroy snarled.

"It's my responsibility as an elected official to lead my classroom," I answered.

"I was handling things just fine—and you are *not* in the classroom now. This is the *real world*. Out here your presidency means nothing." Mr. Pomeroy had gotten red in the face.

I ignored him. "We want to see IDs for all of you.

How will it look on national television—sixth-grade class arrested by *alleged* government agents. Class 6-A abducted from school playground by mysterious people *claiming* to be government agents."

"We are *not* arresting you." Uncle Pat wasn't yelling, but he was near to it.

"And we're certainly *not* abducting you," complained a man in coveralls.

"Who is that kid?" a woman agent asked.

"She's our president," said Helene proudly. She gave Pomeroy a dirty look. "She speaks for all of us. Right, 6-A?"

"Right!"

"Who said anything about television? None of this is going to be on television." A woman holding a clipboard looked around nervously.

"WE DID!" shouted Helene. "What do you think our parents will do when we don't show up after school? They'll call the police, the media, the mayor!"

"I can see it now," said Paul, "headlines—nationwide: SIXTH-GRADE CLASS ARRESTED FOR HAVING MARTIAN TEACHER."

"DOG FROM SPACE GIVES SIXTH GRADERS FLEAS," added Helene.

"He isn't a Martian," said Paul's Uncle Pat.

"That isn't really a dog," said a woman in coveralls.

"More headlines . . . ," I chimed in. ". . . CHILDREN

Given the Third Degree Over Man and Dog from Invisible Spaceship."

"Evening news—" began Aaron.

"That's enough!" shouted Uncle Pat. The government people regrouped near their vehicles and had a conference.

"I wish I were telepathic," I said.

"I wish I were warm. Goldberg's mental blanket seems to be disintegrating," said Ellenbeth, shivering.

The conference broke up. Paul's Uncle Pat came over to us. "We're leaving now. But before we go, we want to be sure you know that discussing this alleged Mr. Fred and his alleged dog will be a breach of national security."

"What is he talking about?" asked someone.

"He's saying that if we go blabbing about Mr. Fred and Duck to anyone, we'll be putting our country in danger," I explained.

"That's stupid."

"Besides, who would believe us?"

"Yeah. *We* weren't sure they were for real, and we were with them for months."

"Can you imagine what people would say if we told them we had a spaceman for a teacher?"

"Not to mention his talking, telepathic spacedog."

"People would think our brains had turned to mush."

"As Mr. Fred said, we have no proof."

"Does this mean you agree to be quiet about what

you've seen—including the unfortunate events of today?" asked Uncle Pat.

We agreed. So did Mr. Pomeroy, who kept looking at his watch. Nothing that had happened seemed to have sunk into his brain as being unusual or strange. A bugged-looking group of failed alien-catchers got into their cars and vans and pulled out of the playground.

Old Bad Breath Pomeroy lined us up and marched us into the building. As we reached our classroom, the bell rang. We turned around and headed toward the door.

"Just where do you delinquents think you're going?"

"To lunch. We're cold and hungry."

"That wasn't the lunch bell. Look at the time."

It was one forty-five. We had missed our meal by almost two hours.

"What happened to the day?" asked Arthur.

"Time sure flies when you're having fun," Helene quipped.

"Don't be a smart-mouth, Miss Holman."

"What did I say wrong, Mr. Pomeroy? That was—" Helene began.

I interrupted. "If we don't get fed, Mr. Pomeroy, we're all going to get sick. It will be a sixth-grade epidemic. Our parents will blame the school for making us stand outside in a freezing blizzard while we were being interrogated by frightening people waving guns." I put my hand to my mouth and coughed.

"Nobody made you stand around on the playground. In fact . . . ," Pomeroy began. "Oh, what's the use? Follow me. I'll make sure you get some hot food. Bring your homework assignments with you so you can keep busy while you wait."

"Good idea, Mr. P.," said Helene. "When we finish our homework, we can spacemail it to Mr. Fred."

"How many times do I have to warn you, Miss Holman?"

"Who's going to teach us tomorrow?" I asked, trying to change the subject.

"Maybe we'll get a Venusian this time," said Mike.

"No, the Venusian's breathing tanks would make it hard to understand what he was saying," said Paul.

"I'd like to have a female space-creature teacher," said Bettina.

"How about it, Old Ba—I mean, Mr. Pomeroy. Do you think you can get us what we're asking for?"

"What were you about to call me, Miss Murray?" Pomeroy gave me a look of doom. I smiled at him and didn't answer. "Line up, 6-A," he ordered. In my head, as we marched to the cafeteria, I could hear someone humming "The Washington Post," Goldberg Fred's favorite Sousa march.

"Did you hear that?" asked Helene as we sat down to wait for the cafeteria crew to heat soup for us.

"The march?" said Alice.

196
*

"Yes," I said. We had all heard it.

"But they've gone home," said Paul.

"Maybe they've changed their minds," I said hopefully. We were silent for a long time, waiting for Mr. Fred to tickle our minds with a thought. Nothing happened. We ate very slowly. By the time we dragged ourselves back to our classroom, it was time to go home.

Maybe Somebody (or Something) Likes a Sixth Grader

19

The next morning, class 6-A gathered in a corner of the playground as far as we could get from the other kids.

"It's funny, but I'm not sad. I mean, I miss them, but I have a feeling," said Alice.

"What kind of feeling?" asked Bettina.

"Sort of like—I don't know—a feeling."

"Well, the only feeling I have is depression," said Arnold. "I miss our space visitors."

"Me, too," said Paul.

"Who cares what you feel?" said Arthur.

"Goldberg Fred said you should forgive me."

"Saying is easy. Doing is not so easy—right, 6-A?" Mike said.

"Right." We all agreed.

"Well, will you try? I didn't mean to make trouble. Goldberg Fred and Duck know that."

"It's a little hard to tell what they know since they're somewhere in deep space by now," said Erica.

Paul looked miserable, but then so did most of the class. I thought a change of subject would help.

"What is that, Alice?" I asked, pointing.

Alice had a bulky, wrapped package wedged between her feet. "A new invention," she said.

"It's a weapon to use against the substitute, isn't it?" I said. "I thought you had learned your lesson."

"It can't hurt anyone—I promise."

"Goldberg Fred believed in nonviolence," said Louise.

"This isn't violent," Alice insisted.

Mr. Pomeroy appeared in front of us. "Line up, 6-A. Follow me." Just to be annoying, we dragged and slumped our way to the top floor.

"Any sign of a teacher?" asked Ellenbeth.

"He couldn't have gotten anyone on such short notice. None of the subs in town will teach us," I said.

"None of the subs in the entire county will come close enough to talk to us," said Alice proudly.

"Maybe in the state," said Mike.

"We're famous," said Arnold.

"I think the word you're looking for is *infamous*," said Ellenbeth.

"I wonder what Pomeroy's going to do with us," said Kathy.

"Maybe he'll take over himself until Christmas," I said.

"He'll never last," said Kathy.

"Vacation is only three days away," I said.

"He'll never last," we all said together.

"Maybe he'll send us home early."

"Three days is *very* early."

"Our parents will have fits."

"*Then* what?" I mused.

"Then what what?" asked Helene.

"Then what do we do for the rest of the year? I liked learning stuff," I whispered.

"Why are you whispering?" Helene asked.

"So *he* can't hear me." I pointed to Pomeroy, who had been ignoring us.

"He doesn't seem to care."

Pomeroy looked unusually happy for a man being forced to deal with 6-A at close quarters for three days. As soon as we were seated, he began speaking. "A miracle has happened. A fine teacher with excellent credentials contacted me last night. I interviewed her early this morning and hired her on the spot. The miracle is that she seems to have heard all about you and is *still* willing to come here and teach. Her specialty is sixth grade, so nothing you do will surprise her.

"She's getting her teaching equipment from her car.

She will be here momentarily." Pomeroy started to leave.

"Teaching equipment?"

"Like handcuffs and chains?"

"I don't think that's allowed in the United States."

"This isn't the United States. It's school." Pomeroy turned and smiled at us.

"What's her name?" someone asked.

"Uh, well . . ." Pomeroy patted his pockets as though looking for something. "I'll let her introduce herself." The bell rang, and he scurried off mumbling something about a meeting.

"Let's do the top-drawer trap first," Louise suggested.

"Do we have time?" asked Mike as he folded some paper into airplanes.

"Not really, Mr. Carson." A tall woman wrapped in layers of scarves and sweaters clunked into the room, banging the burlap shopping bags she was carrying against the ragged edges of what was left of the broken classroom door.

"Someone really should repair this door or at least remove the debris from the frame!" she shouted into the hallway. Then she kind of swung the bags onto the teacher's desk, pushed her thick eyeglasses back from the tip of her nose where they were about to fall to the floor, and hiked up the waistband of her skirt. She was a fairly sloppy-looking person.

"No wonder she was willing to teach us. Who else would have her?" giggled Helene.

"On the other hand, Ms. Holman, who else would have all of you?"

Helene blushed. "I didn't think she could hear me," she whispered to me.

"In order to reach a sixth-grade mind, one must cope with the body—a large part of which seems to be mouth. Acute hearing on the part of the sixth-grade teacher is a precious advantage."

"She heard me again," said Helene, slumping in her chair.

Without looking at us, the teacher walked around the edge of the room examining our work.

Helene poked me. "She knew my name." Helene's lips moved, but no sound came from her mouth.

"Mine, too," mimed Mike.

"Have either of you ever met her before?" I asked. They both shook their heads.

"This is definitely weird," said Alice, out loud, writing something in the class logbook.

The teacher smiled a warm and friendly smile at her. Alice put away the log. When the teacher passed Mike's desk, she picked up a plane, gave it a couple of extra folds, and sailed it into the air. It did two full loops before landing next to a shopping bag.

"A simple matter of aerodynamics," she said.

"It couldn't be," I whispered.

"Impossible," whispered Paul.

"I don't think she's local," said Helene.

"It's a coincidence," said Ellenbeth. "It is a well-known fact that many people insist that there are no such phenomena as coincidences, however, I recently saw a documentary called—"

"What is Ellenbeth talking about?" interrupted Arthur.

"She's saying that it doesn't mean anything that this teacher knows our names and can make and sail paper airplanes like Mr. Fred," I explained.

"Oh," said Arthur.

"Ellenbeth never believes anything until it's on public television," Mike complained.

"That's not true," Ellenbeth insisted.

The teacher walked to the board and picked up a piece of chalk. "My name is Montaña Dale Sierra." She wrote as she spoke. "You may call me Ms. Sierra."

"Your name sounds like some sort of hiking club," Helene said.

"I enjoy the outdoors, Ms. Holman."

"Wait a second," said Ellenbeth, "just wait one second." Ellenbeth rushed into the back room.

"An enterprising child." Montaña Dale Sierra walked behind the teacher's desk and began emptying the contents of one of her shopping bags into the drawers.

An out-of-breath Ellenbeth skidded back into the room waving a book in the air. "I've got it!" she announced.

"What?" we all asked.

"I remembered from a program I saw that Montaña means mountain. I found the book we were using to research the meaning of names when we were working on the Challenge. Guess what Sierra means?" Ellenbeth stopped to take a breath.

"What?" we all asked.

"It means mountain," she said dramatically.

We all looked blankly at Ellenbeth.

"Don't you get it?"

"Get what?"

"Ellenbeth's gone over the deep end."

"I think you mean over the edge."

"Whatever."

"SIERRA MEANS MOUNTAIN, TOO!" Ellenbeth was red in the face from exasperation.

"So?"

"So Dale means valley." Ellenbeth waved the little book in the air. "This person claims her name is Mountain Valley Mountain. See?"

"This person says her name is Montaña Dale Sierra, not Mountain Valley Mountain," said Kathy.

"See what?" asked Arnold.

"This book says that all three names can be first or last

names. So a person whose name is Montaña Sierra could be named Sierra Montaña."

"Or Dale Montaña . . ."

"Or Sierra Dale . . ."

"Or Montaña Dale . . ."

"Or . . ."

"You're all totally dense." Ellenbeth put the name book into her desk and slammed down the top.

"Maybe her parents like outdoor names," Arthur suggested.

"If you're trying to make a case, you're failing, Ellenbeth. Goldberg Fred didn't have two last names—he had a last name first," said Bettina.

"This is trickier. It is a last name first, no matter how you arrange it," Ellenbeth insisted.

"She's got a point," I said. "And this Ms. Sierra does have very sharp hearing—if you know what I mean."

"And she did know our names," said Mike.

"Maybe she's just someone whose parents appreciated the ups and downs of life," said Helene. Everyone stared at her. "That was a joke. Mountain, valley, mountain— ups and downs—get it? Oh boy, I think I'm losing it."

"I'll call the roll now." Ms. Sierra interrupted the silence. "Aaron Zipler," she began.

"It *is* another one," I said.

"No doubt about it," said Paul.

"You going to turn this one in, too, Paul?" asked Alice, unwrapping her invention.

Paul pretended not to hear.

"Watch this," whispered Alice as she loaded a foam ball into a thing that looked like a cross between a catapult and a bow and arrow. She aimed and shot. The foam ball arched in the air and headed directly for Ms. Sierra, who was reading the roll book.

Watch this, said a voice inside our heads. The ball stopped inches from Ms. Sierra's face, reversed direction, and headed back toward Alice. Alice ducked under her desk. The ball followed her and bounced up and down on her back before falling to the floor.

Nyice, nee-eet. A second voice whined in our brains. We looked at each other and then at Montaña Sierra.

"That was my friend Wolf." Ms. Sierra poked one of the shopping bags and a large cat stepped daintily onto the desk.

"A Frinch Puddle cat?" said Paul.

"A Boomese Tree cat," corrected Ms. Sierra.

Heeeeee. Heeeeee, mewed the telepathic cat voice. *No cats in Frence.*

"So I guess he doesn't specialize in catching Puddle Sharks," I said.

"*She* will someday be a world-class Tree Sharker—it's in her genes. Right now Wolf is but a kitten."

"*That's* a kitten? How big is she going to get?" asked Mike.

"Exactly where are you from?" I asked.

"Mr. Fred told me about your single-mindedness, Ms. Murray."

"You've seen Mr. Fred? Where?"

"Around. He sends his regards. Now to business. We'll plan the next step of the Challenge as soon as you get your usual nonsense out of your systems. Go to it." Montaña Sierra sat down, tilted her chair against the board, and closed her eyes.

An airplane sailed toward Wolf, who shredded it mid-air. Our class runners tore around the room. Kids sang and made confetti and stomped their feet on the floor. But this time it was different. We weren't angry. We weren't sad. We were celebrating. It had happened again. We were the luckiest kids in the universe.

"She's another teacher from space," I shouted. "Maybe we're being invaded. Maybe the government people were right! Maybe they're everywhere!"

"I hope so!" Helene proclaimed. She gave a whoop and jumped off her chair.

"Actually, on Earth we're only in sixth-grade classes," Montaña Sierra opened one eye and shouted above the din.

"Maybe Goldberg Fred sent her to kidnap one of us," said Paul.

"I hope it's me," said Shaundra.

"Why should they want you?" asked Arthur.

"I'm a very resourceful and intelligent kid—a good example of a human being," Shaundra answered.

"If *all* they wanted was a good example of a human, they'd take someone who is so average and ordinary that the person would be totally boring—like Lucile," said Ellenbeth.

"Me? I don't want to be kidnapped," Lucy cringed.

"It's probably called spacenapping," Arnold suggested.

"And they'll probably return you—after a while," Mike added.

"After just a few experiments," said Alice.

"Ohhhhhhh," Lucy moaned.

"Stop worrying, Lucy. This Montaña Sierra didn't say anything about taking one of us for a space ride," I said.

"She didn't say anything about *not* taking us for a space ride," Lucy countered.

"If you're so smart, why is she here, Anya?" asked Paul.

"Who, Lucy?" I asked innocently.

"You know who."

"To teach, I guess, like Goldberg Fred."

"Why would anyone travel thousands of light-years just to teach a sixth-grade class?"

"Cheap rocket fuel?" Helene suggested. A few people tittered. Helene was back on the funny track.

Actually, we who travel and teach do so under the auspices of the USGTEP—the Universal Sixth-Grade Teacher Exchange Program.

"Telepathy alert," said Helene, covering her ears.

"It was in my head, too," I said.

"Mine, too," said Erica, smiling.

"If a planet sends teachers to Earth, do Earth teachers get to go to the planet? That's what exchange means, doesn't it?" Alice asked.

"Thinking of becoming a teacher, Alice?" asked Mike.

"Why not? I love to travel."

Your Miss Cintron went to South America. I've come to My Dear Watson Elementary School. That's an exchange of services, don't you think? said the voice in our heads.

You're not from South America. Where are you from, exactly? I thought back. I was beginning to like talking without speaking.

Oh, around. I've moved a great deal. I, too, love to travel.

This time I'm going to find out exactly where "around" is, I thought. You couldn't be half as slimy or tricky as Goldberg Fred.

Want to bet? He's my baby brother. I taught him everything he knows.

How come you don't have the same last name? I thought.

I could be married—or he could be married—or perhaps we simply have different naming customs. I can assure you, Goldy is my little brother.

Goldy? I thought.

"Do you think she's telling the truth?" asked Helene.

"You heard that?"

"I heard the whole conversation."

"You heard *me* in your head?" I gasped.

"Me, too," said Bettina. "I heard everything." The class was suddenly quiet. They had all heard. For a few minutes I, Anya Murray, class president of 6-A, had been truly telepathic.

"We have miles to go before we sleep," said Montaña Dale Sierra. "Let's get to work."

Helene came home with me that day.

"You know what the best part is?" I asked.

"We're going to keep learning a whole lot."

"No."

"Montaña Sierra will turn out to be funnier than her brother."

"No."

"We'll get to go through a portal this time," said Paul, who was tagging along.

"No."

"She's going to teach us to use telepathy—with everyone," said Helene.

"No."

"Then what?"

"I think there are people who actually like sixth graders."

"What people?"

"Sixth-grade exchange teachers from space."

"But they're not human. Do they count?"

"They have to. For now, they're all we've got."